W9-BBL-553
3 4028 09321 9153
HARRIS COUNTY PUBLIC LIBRARY

J 741.597 How
Howard, Tini
Barbie video game hero. #1,
 Need for speed

DISCARD                    $7.99
on1003719011

# VIDEO HERO #1

## Need For Speed

PAPERCUTZ

Edit,
Buller,
Paws Inc.

# MORE GREAT GRAPHIC NOVEL SERIES AVAILABLE FROM PAPERCUTZ

**BARBIE #1**

**BARBIE PUPPY PARTY**

**BARBIE #2**

**BARBIE STARLIGHT ADVENTURE**

**FUZZY BASEBALL**

**THE GARFIELD SHOW #6**

**DISNEY FAIRIES #18**

**MINNIE & DAISY #1**

**NANCY DREW DIARIES #7**

**THE RED SHOES**

**SCARLETT**

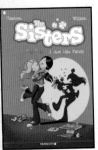
**THE SISTERS #1**

**THE WILD SMURF**

**THEA STILTON #6**

**TROLLS #1**

THE SMURFS, MINNIE & DAISY, DISNEY FAIRIES, THE GARFIELD SHOW, BARBIE and TROLLS graphic novels are available for $7.99 in paperback, and $12.99 in hardcover. THEA STILTON graphic novels are available for $9.99 in hardcover only. FUZZY BASEBALL and NANCY DREW DIARIES graphic novels are available for $9.99 in paperback only. THE LUNCH WITCH, SCARLETT, and ANNE OF GREEN BAGELS graphic novels are available for $14.99 in paperback only. THE RED SHOES graphic novel is available for $12.99 in hardcover only. Available from booksellers everywhere. You can also order online from www.papercutz.com. Or call 1-800-886-1223, Monday through Friday, 9–5 EST. MC, Visa, and AmEx accepted. To order by mail, please add $4.00 for postage and handling for first book ordered, $1.00 for each additional book and make check payable to NBM Publishing. Send to: Papercutz, 160 Broadway, Suite 700, East Wing, New York, NY 10038.

THE SMURFS, THE GARFIELD SHOW, BARBIE, TROLLS, THEA STILTON, FUZZY BASEBALL, THE LUNCH WITCH, NANCY DREW DIARIES, THE RED SHOES, ANNE OF GREEN BAGELS, and SCARLETT graphic novels are also available wherever e-books are sold.

BARBIE ©2017 Mattel; DREAMWORKS TROLLS ©2017 DreamWorks Animation LLC. All Rights Reserved; LUNCH WITCH ©2017 Deb Lucke; DISN ... RIES, DISNEY GRAPHIC NOVELS, MINNIE & DAISY; ©2017 Disney Enterprises, Inc.; THEA STILTON; ©2017 Atlantyca S.p.A; SCARLETT ©2017 Ba ... ns, 2013; THE RED SHOES ©2017 Metaphrog; FUZZY BASEBALL ©2017 by John Steven Gurney; ANNE OF GREEN BAGELS ©2017 by Je ... and Susan Schade; "THE GARFIELD SHOW" series ©2017 Dargaud Media. All rights reserved. © Paws. "Garfield" & Garfield characters TM ... NANCY DREW DIARIES ©2017 by Simon & Schuster, Inc.

© Peyo - 2017 - Licensed through Lafig Belgium - www.s...

# Barbie™ VIDEO GAME HERO #1™

**Story by Tini Howard**
**Art by Jules Rivera**

PAPERCUTZ™

NEW YORK

**Barbie VIDEO GAME HERO** #1

BARBIE VIDEO GAME HERO #1 "Need for Speed"
Tini Howard – Writer
Jules Rivera – Artist
Laurie Smith – Colorist (cover)
Ronda Pattison – Colorist
Janice Chiang – Letterer

Grace Ilori – Production
Mariah McCourt – Editor
Jeff Whitman - Assistant Managing Editor
Beth Scorzato – Special Thanks
Jim Salicrup
Editor-in-Chief

Papercutz books may be purchased for business or pro-motional use. For information on bulk purchases please contact Macmillan Corporate and Premium Sales Depart-ment at (800) 221-7945 x5442.

ISBN: 978-162991-644-6 hardcover edition
ISBN: 978-162991-643-9 paperback edition

Printed in China
September 2017

Distributed by Macmillan
First Printing

© 2017 Mattel. All Rights Reserved.

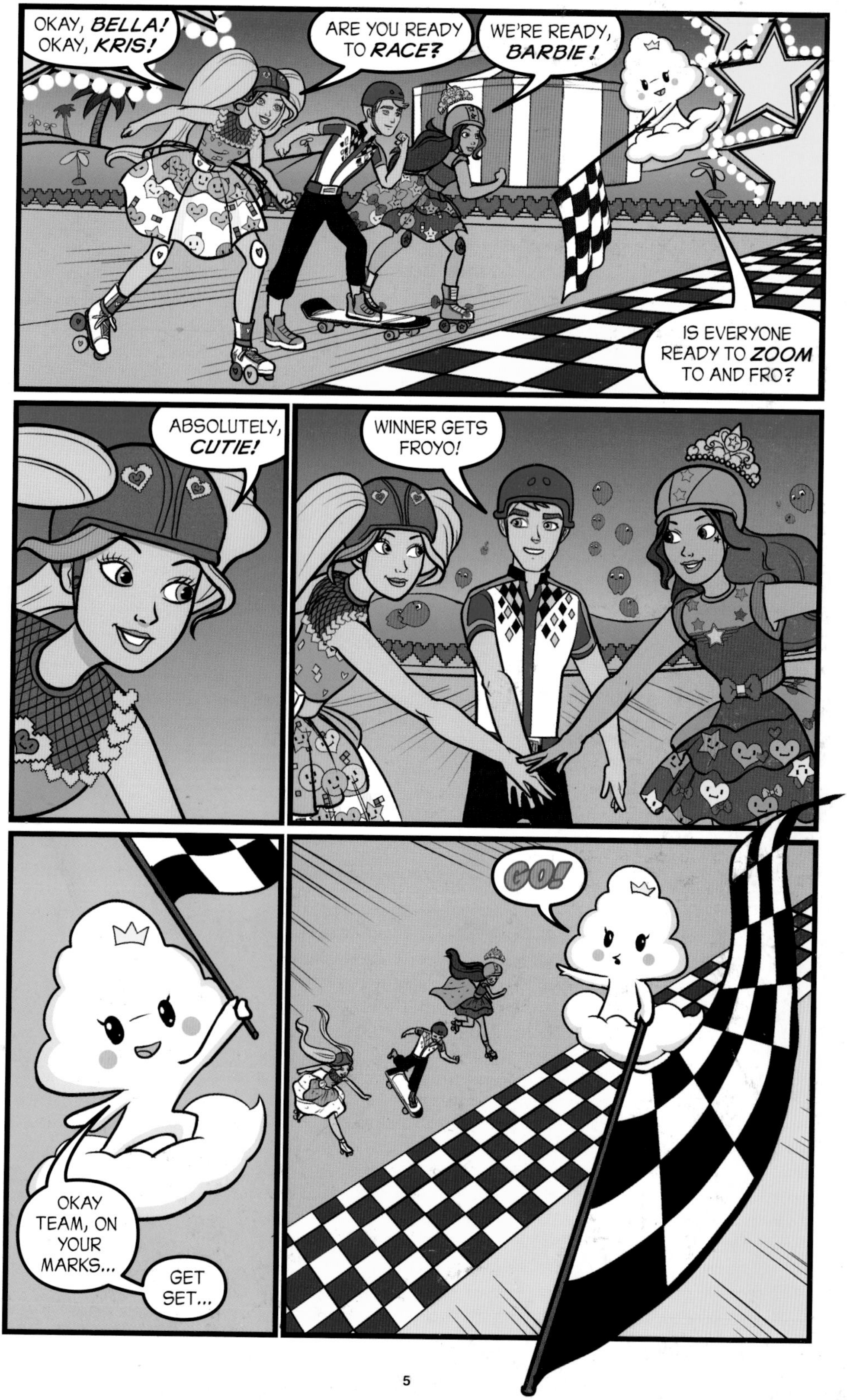

OKAY, BELLA! OKAY, KRIS!
ARE YOU READY TO RACE?
WE'RE READY, BARBIE!
IS EVERYONE READY TO ZOOM TO AND FRO?
ABSOLUTELY, CUTIE!
WINNER GETS FROYO!
OKAY TEAM, ON YOUR MARKS...
GET SET...
GO!

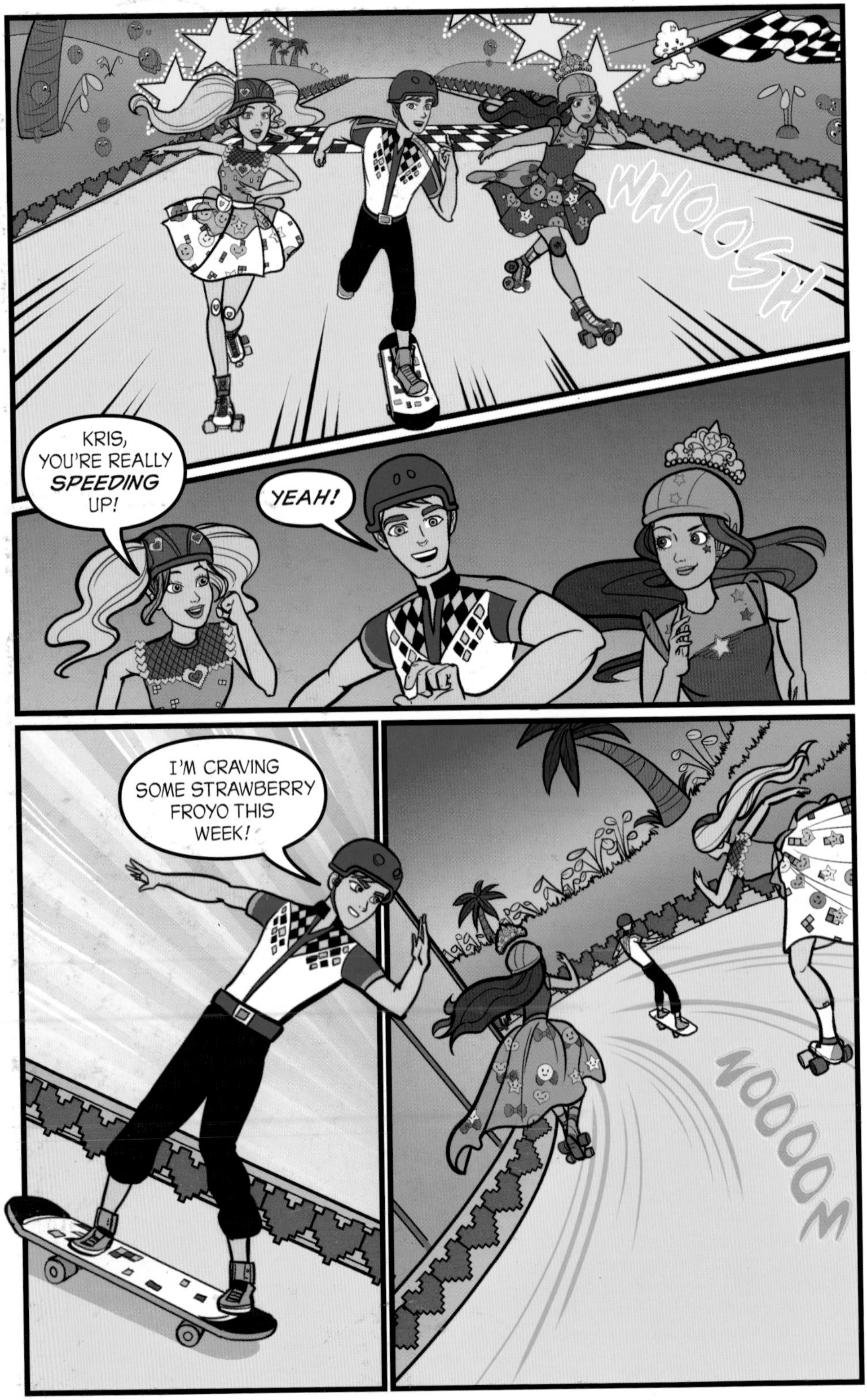
WHOOSH
KRIS, YOU'RE REALLY SPEEDING UP!
YEAH!
I'M CRAVING SOME STRAWBERRY FROYO THIS WEEK!
NOOOOOM

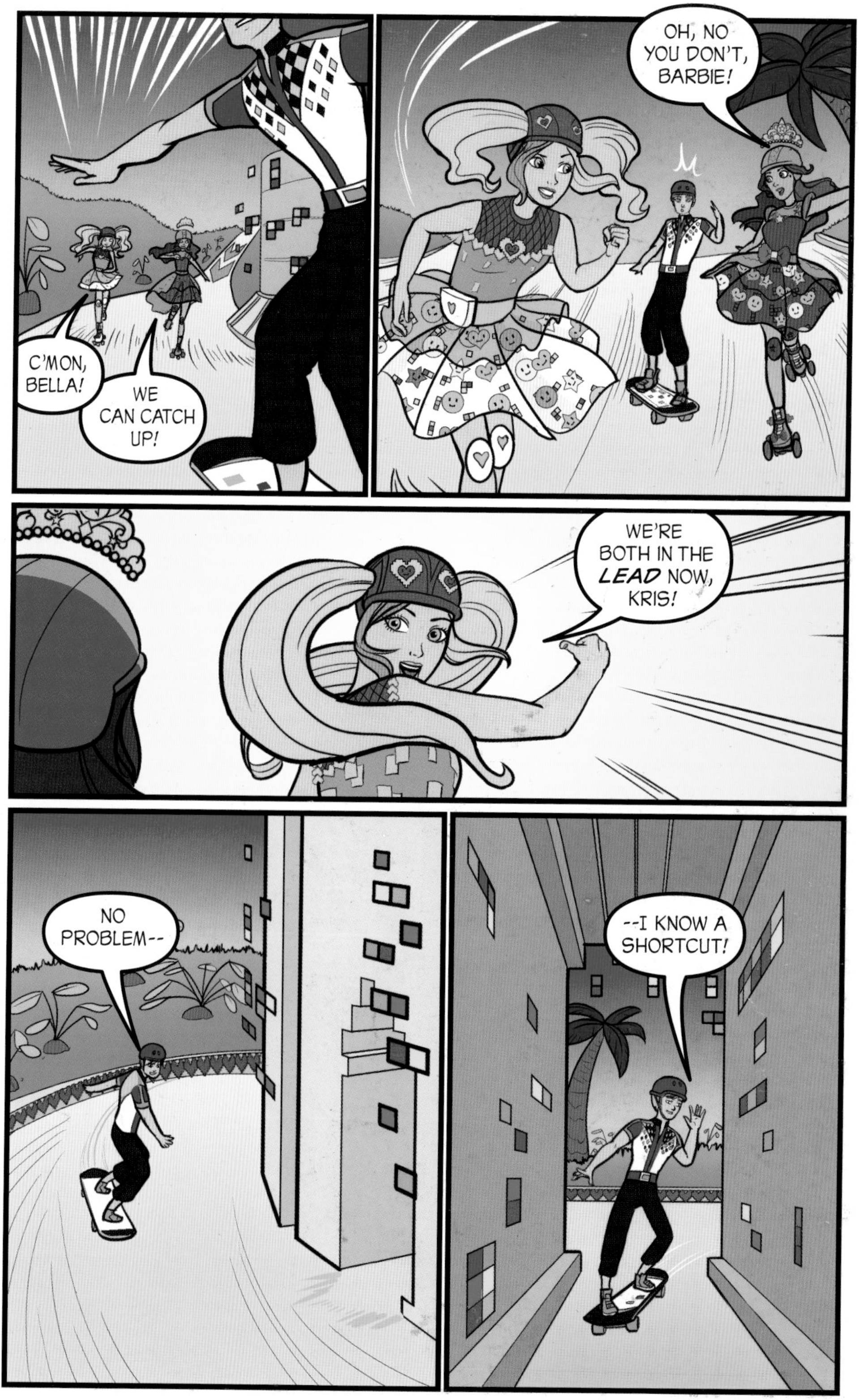
C'MON, BELLA!
WE CAN CATCH UP!
OH, NO YOU DON'T, BARBIE!
WE'RE BOTH IN THE *LEAD* NOW, KRIS!
NO PROBLEM--
--I KNOW A SHORTCUT!

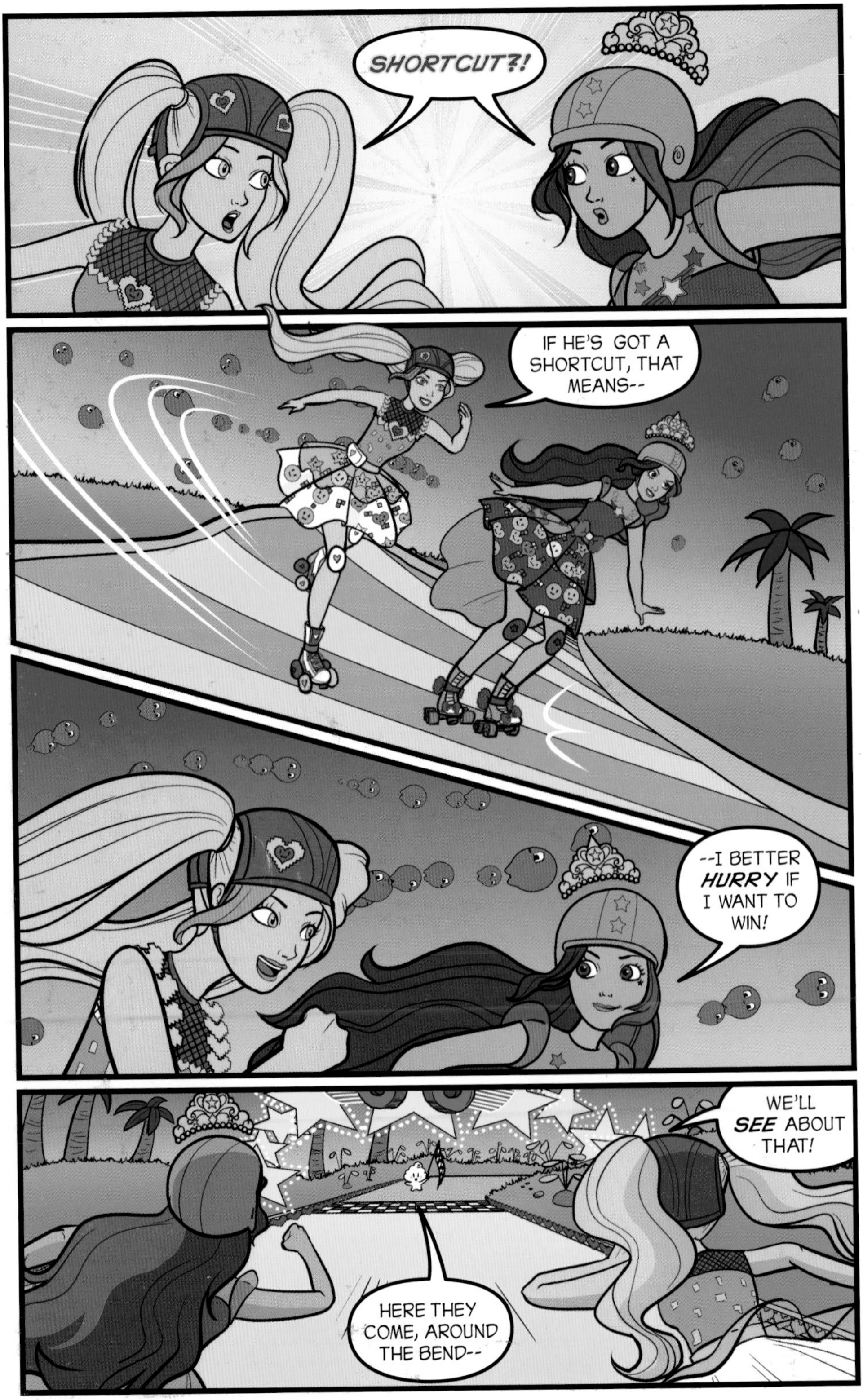
SHORTCUT?!
IF HE'S GOT A SHORTCUT, THAT MEANS--
--I BETTER HURRY IF I WANT TO WIN!
WE'LL SEE ABOUT THAT!
HERE THEY COME, AROUND THE BEND--

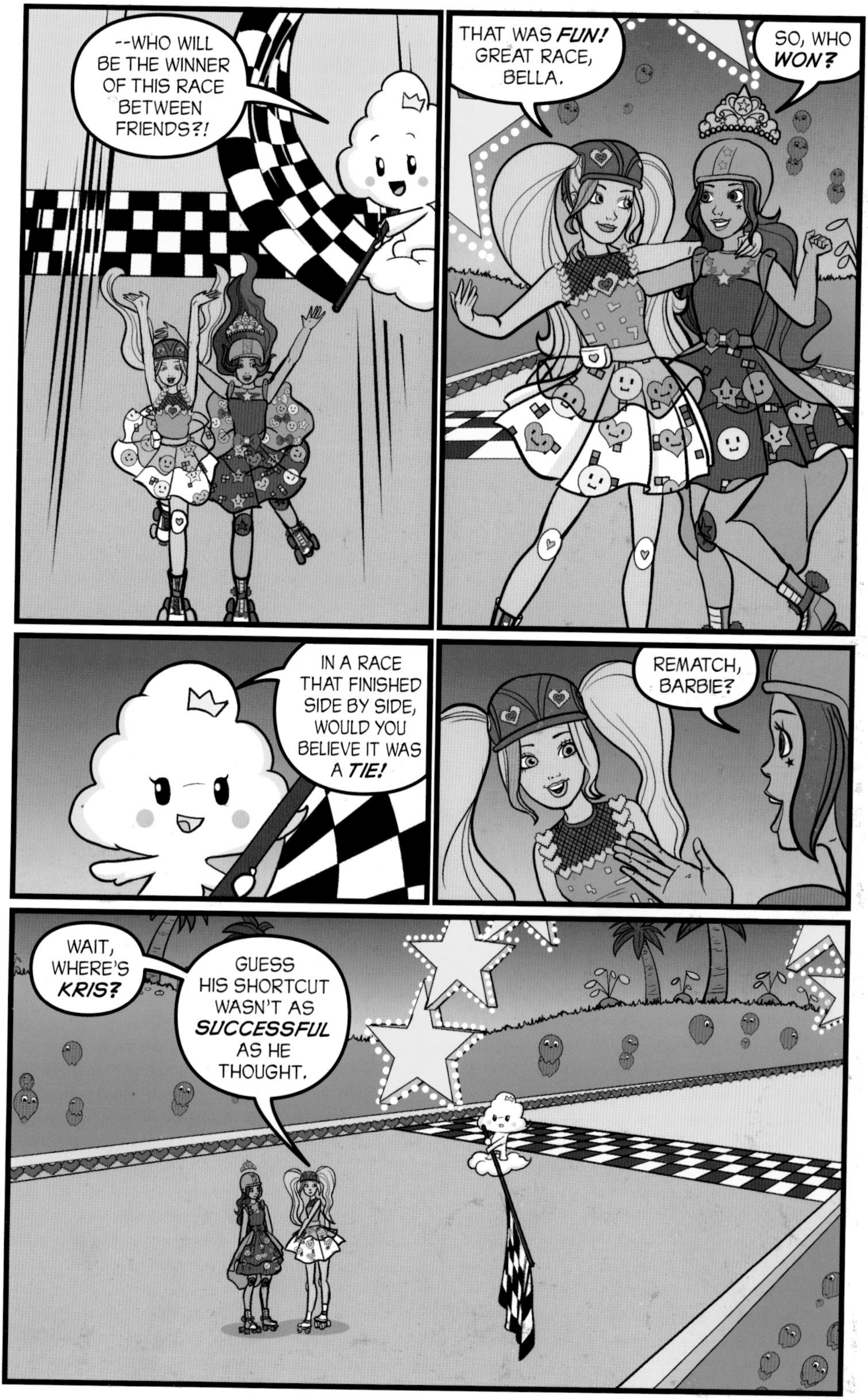
--WHO WILL BE THE WINNER OF THIS RACE BETWEEN FRIENDS?!
THAT WAS FUN! GREAT RACE, BELLA.
SO, WHO WON?
IN A RACE THAT FINISHED SIDE BY SIDE, WOULD YOU BELIEVE IT WAS A TIE!
REMATCH, BARBIE?
WAIT, WHERE'S KRIS?
GUESS HIS SHORTCUT WASN'T AS SUCCESSFUL AS HE THOUGHT.

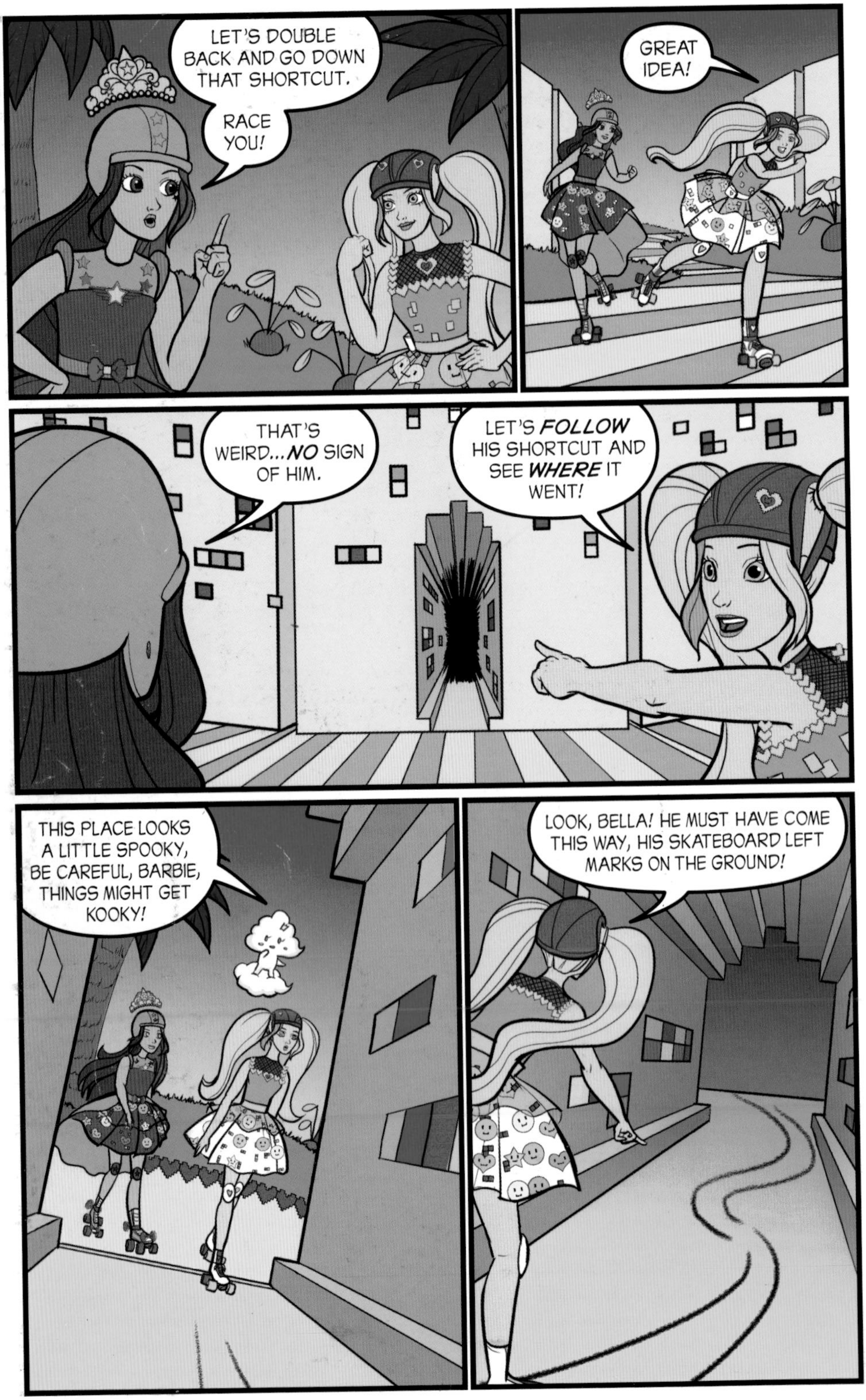
LET'S DOUBLE BACK AND GO DOWN THAT SHORTCUT.
RACE YOU!
GREAT IDEA!
THAT'S WEIRD...NO SIGN OF HIM.
LET'S FOLLOW HIS SHORTCUT AND SEE WHERE IT WENT!
THIS PLACE LOOKS A LITTLE SPOOKY, BE CAREFUL, BARBIE, THINGS MIGHT GET KOOKY!
LOOK, BELLA! HE MUST HAVE COME THIS WAY, HIS SKATEBOARD LEFT MARKS ON THE GROUND!

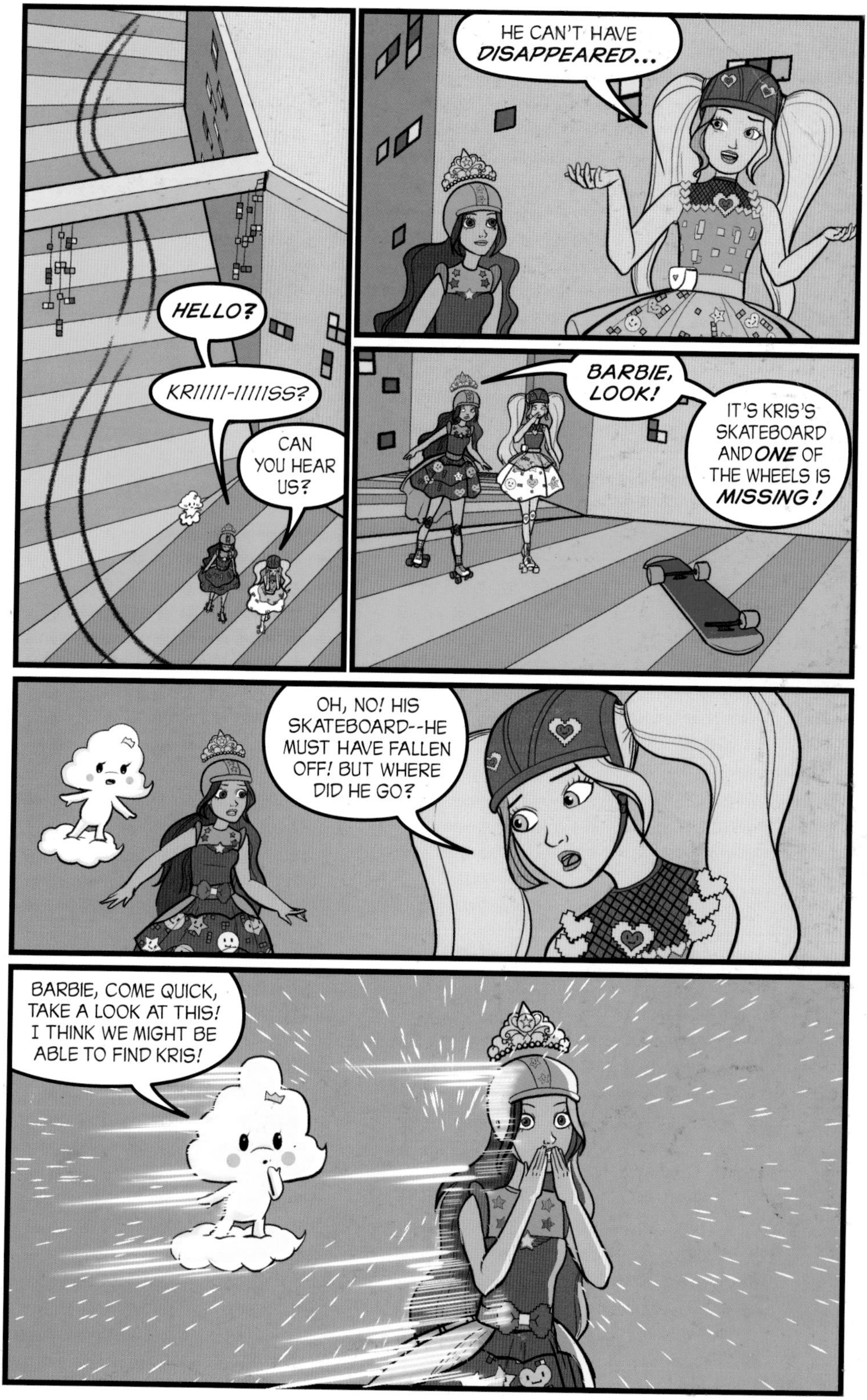
HELLO?
KRIIIII-IIIIISS?
CAN YOU HEAR US?
HE CAN'T HAVE DISAPPEARED...
BARBIE, LOOK!
IT'S KRIS'S SKATEBOARD AND ONE OF THE WHEELS IS MISSING!
OH, NO! HIS SKATEBOARD--HE MUST HAVE FALLEN OFF! BUT WHERE DID HE GO?
BARBIE, COME QUICK, TAKE A LOOK AT THIS! I THINK WE MIGHT BE ABLE TO FIND KRIS!

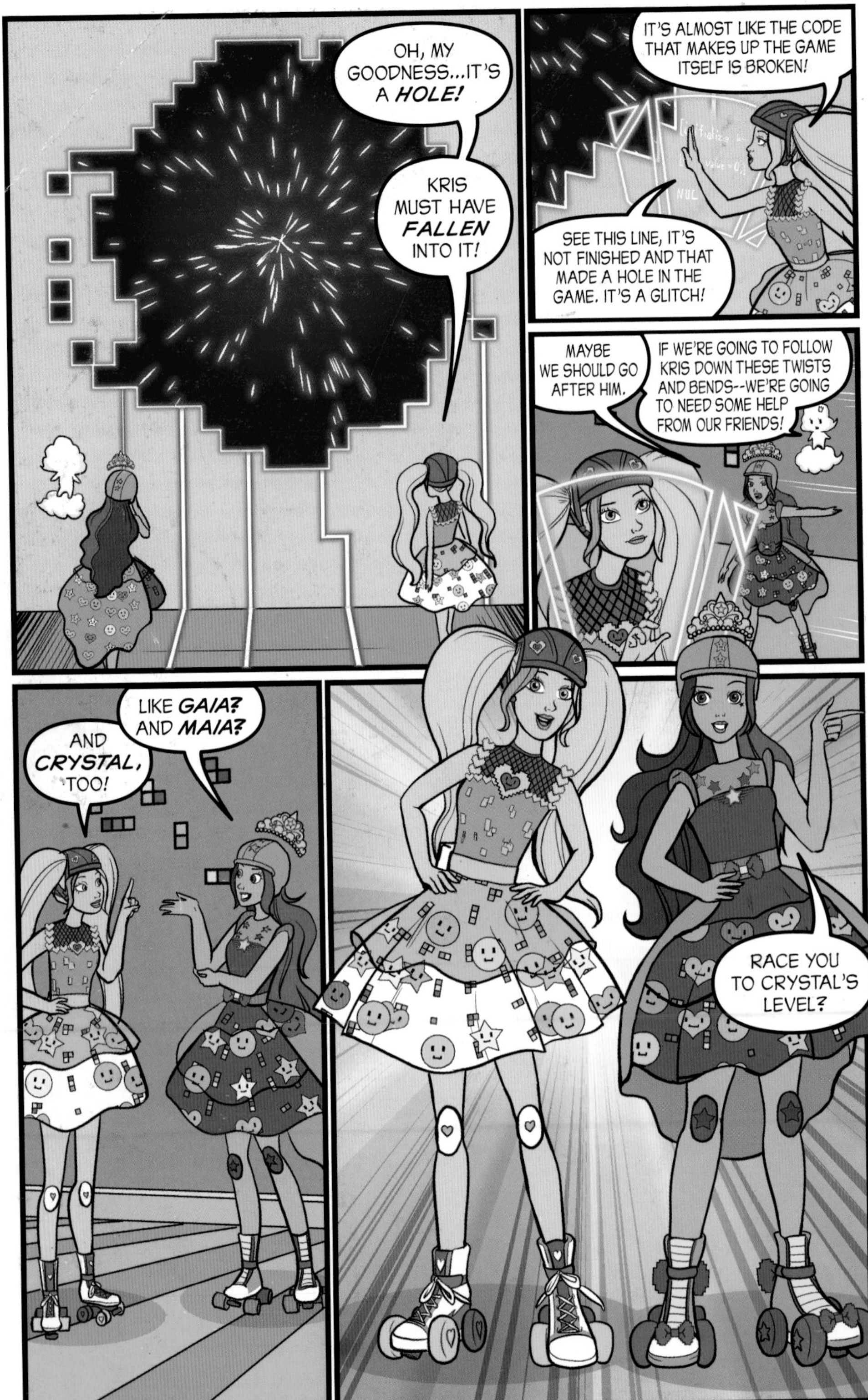
OH, MY GOODNESS...IT'S A HOLE!
KRIS MUST HAVE FALLEN INTO IT!
IT'S ALMOST LIKE THE CODE THAT MAKES UP THE GAME ITSELF IS BROKEN!
SEE THIS LINE, IT'S NOT FINISHED AND THAT MADE A HOLE IN THE GAME. IT'S A GLITCH!
MAYBE WE SHOULD GO AFTER HIM.
IF WE'RE GOING TO FOLLOW KRIS DOWN THESE TWISTS AND BENDS--WE'RE GOING TO NEED SOME HELP FROM OUR FRIENDS!
LIKE GAIA? AND MAIA?
AND CRYSTAL, TOO!
RACE YOU TO CRYSTAL'S LEVEL?

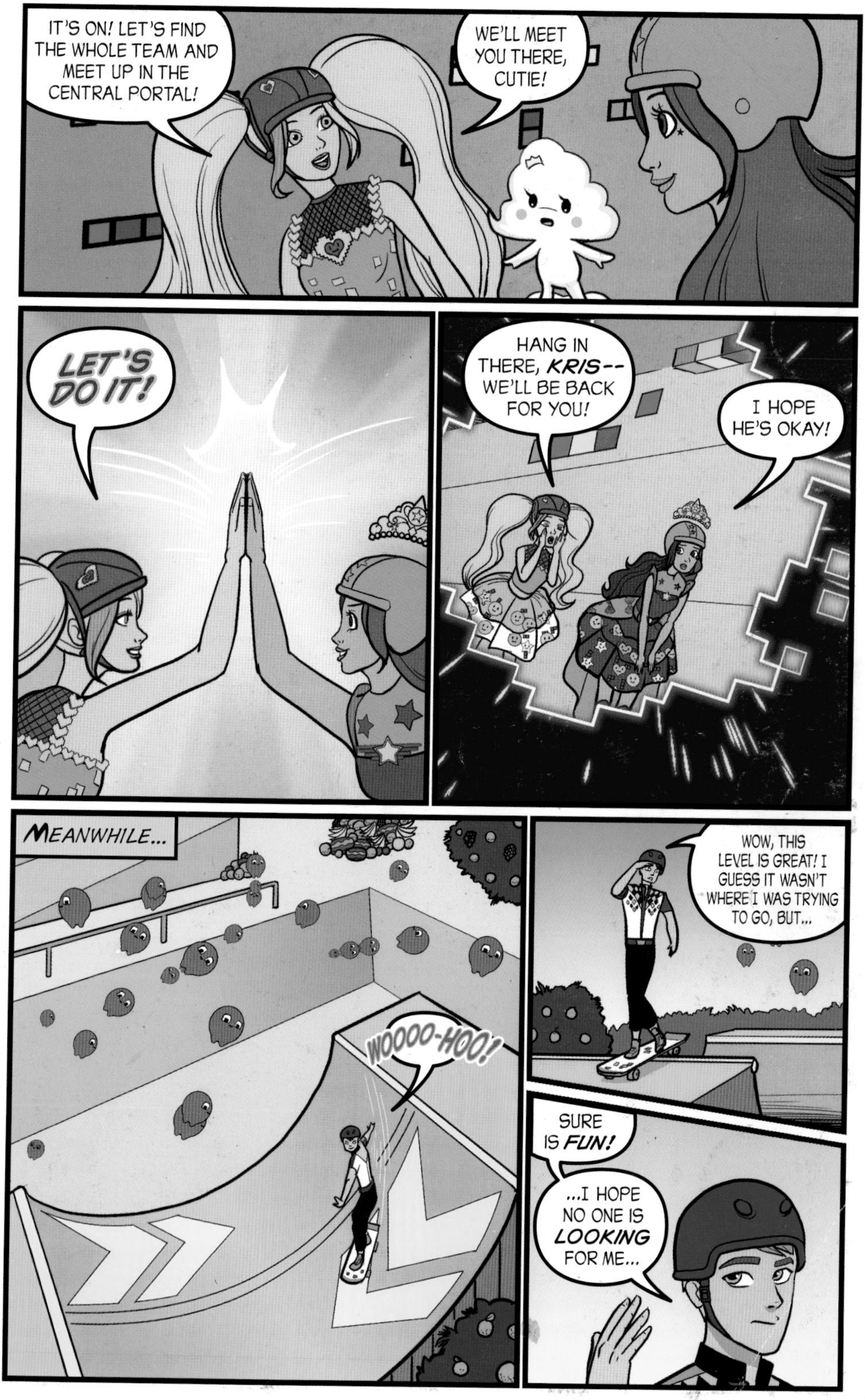
IT'S ON! LET'S FIND THE WHOLE TEAM AND MEET UP IN THE CENTRAL PORTAL!
WE'LL MEET YOU THERE, CUTIE!
LET'S DO IT!
HANG IN THERE, KRIS-- WE'LL BE BACK FOR YOU!
I HOPE HE'S OKAY!
MEANWHILE...
WOOOO-HOO!
WOW, THIS LEVEL IS GREAT! I GUESS IT WASN'T WHERE I WAS TRYING TO GO, BUT...
SURE IS FUN!
...I HOPE NO ONE IS LOOKING FOR ME...

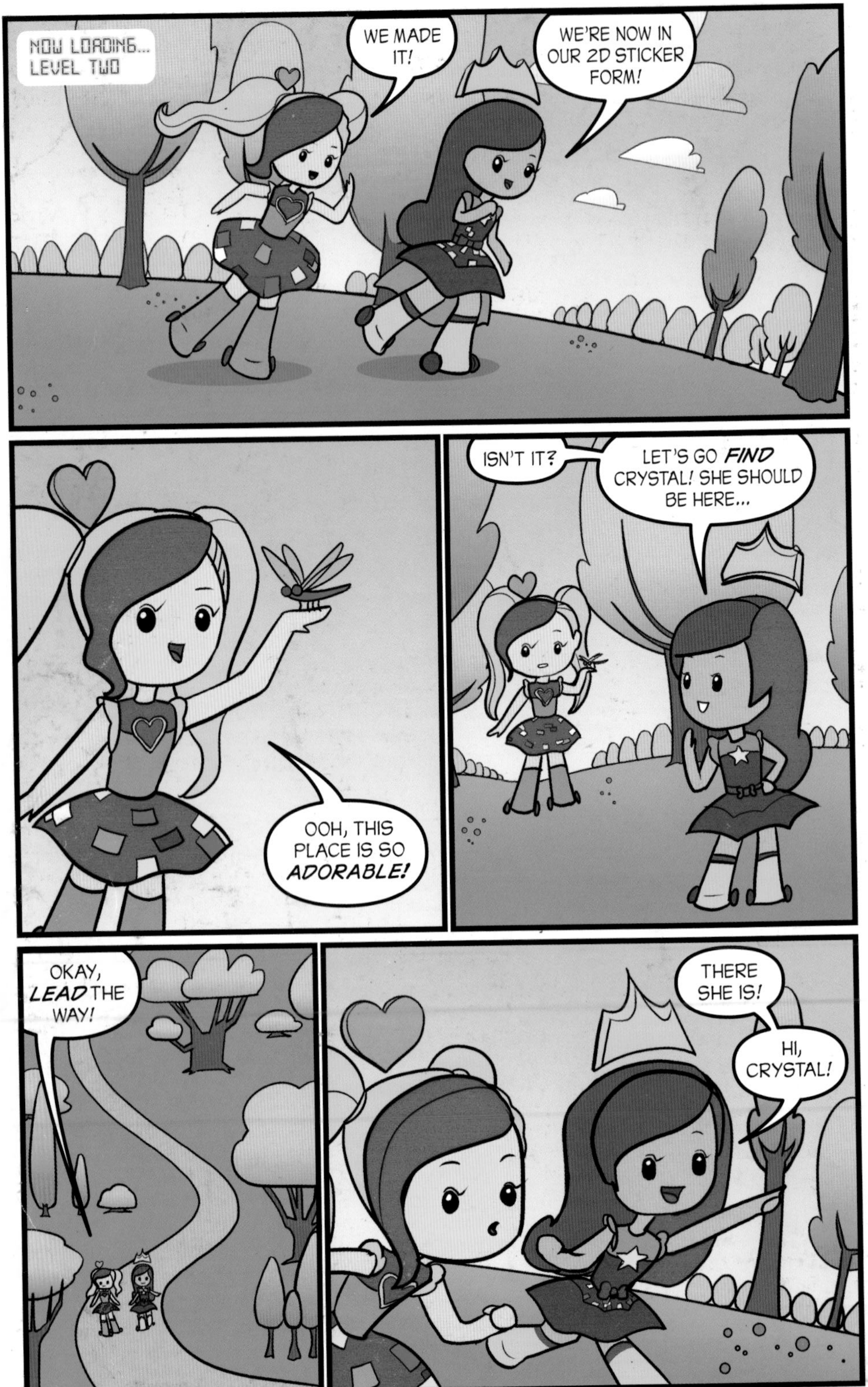
NOW LOADING...
LEVEL TWO
WE MADE IT!
WE'RE NOW IN OUR 2D STICKER FORM!
OOH, THIS PLACE IS SO ADORABLE!
ISN'T IT?
LET'S GO FIND CRYSTAL! SHE SHOULD BE HERE...
OKAY, LEAD THE WAY!
THERE SHE IS!
HI, CRYSTAL!

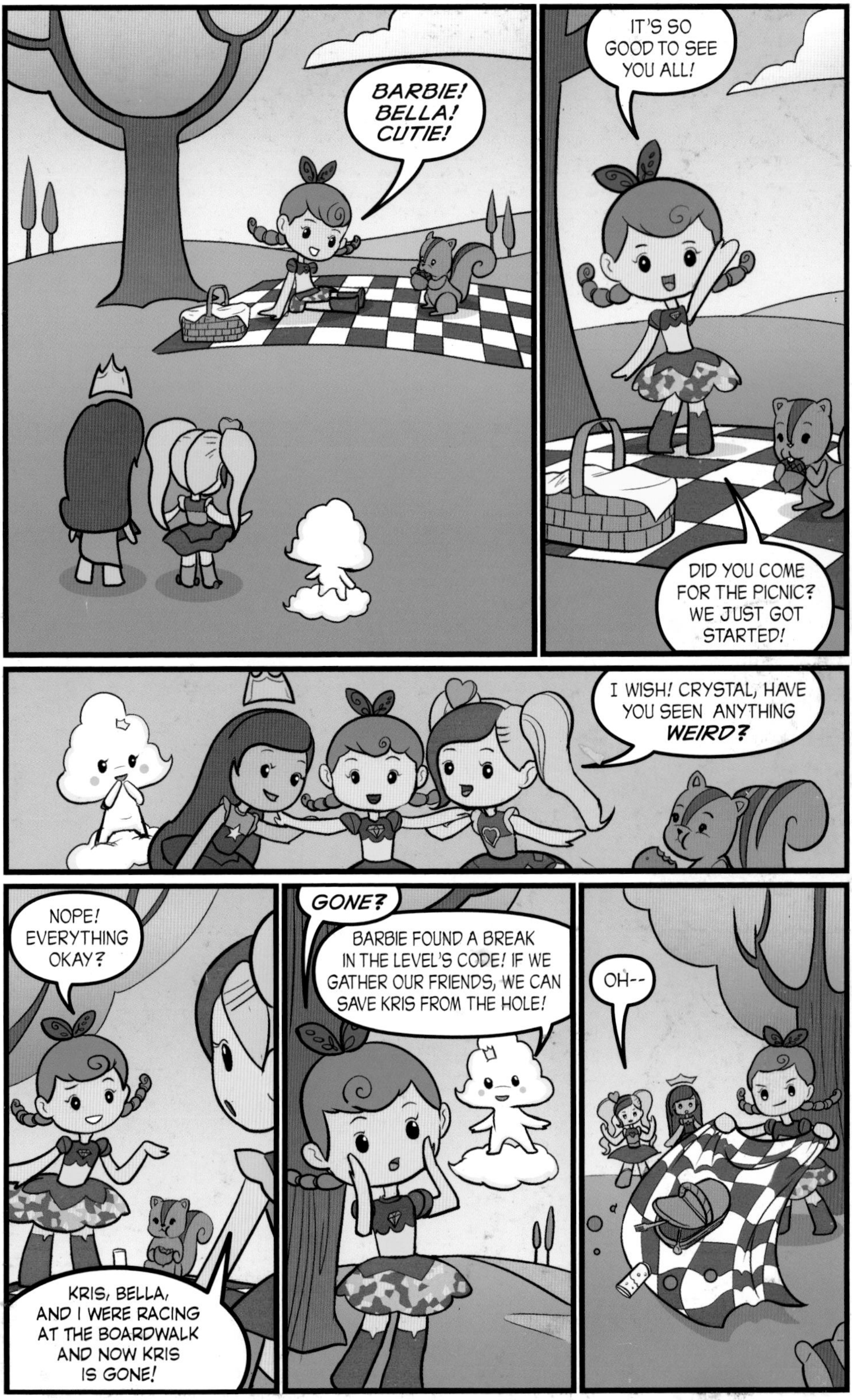
BARBIE! BELLA! CUTIE!
IT'S SO GOOD TO SEE YOU ALL!
DID YOU COME FOR THE PICNIC? WE JUST GOT STARTED!
I WISH! CRYSTAL, HAVE YOU SEEN ANYTHING WEIRD?
NOPE! EVERYTHING OKAY?
KRIS, BELLA, AND I WERE RACING AT THE BOARDWALK AND NOW KRIS IS GONE!
GONE?
BARBIE FOUND A BREAK IN THE LEVEL'S CODE! IF WE GATHER OUR FRIENDS, WE CAN SAVE KRIS FROM THE HOLE!
OH--

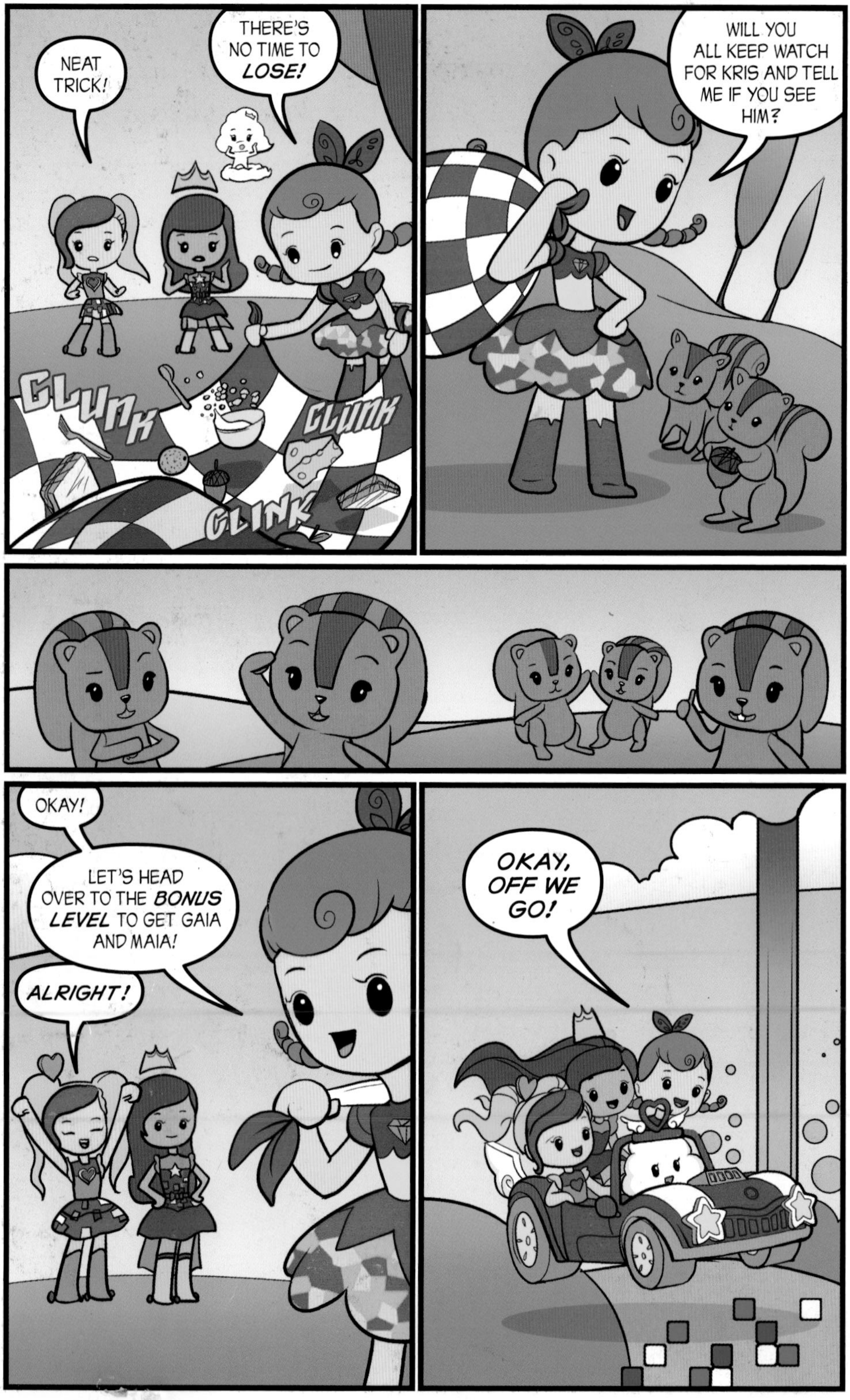
NEAT TRICK!
THERE'S NO TIME TO LOSE!
CLUNK
CLUNK
CLINK
WILL YOU ALL KEEP WATCH FOR KRIS AND TELL ME IF YOU SEE HIM?
OKAY!
LET'S HEAD OVER TO THE BONUS LEVEL TO GET GAIA AND MAIA!
ALRIGHT!
OKAY, OFF WE GO!

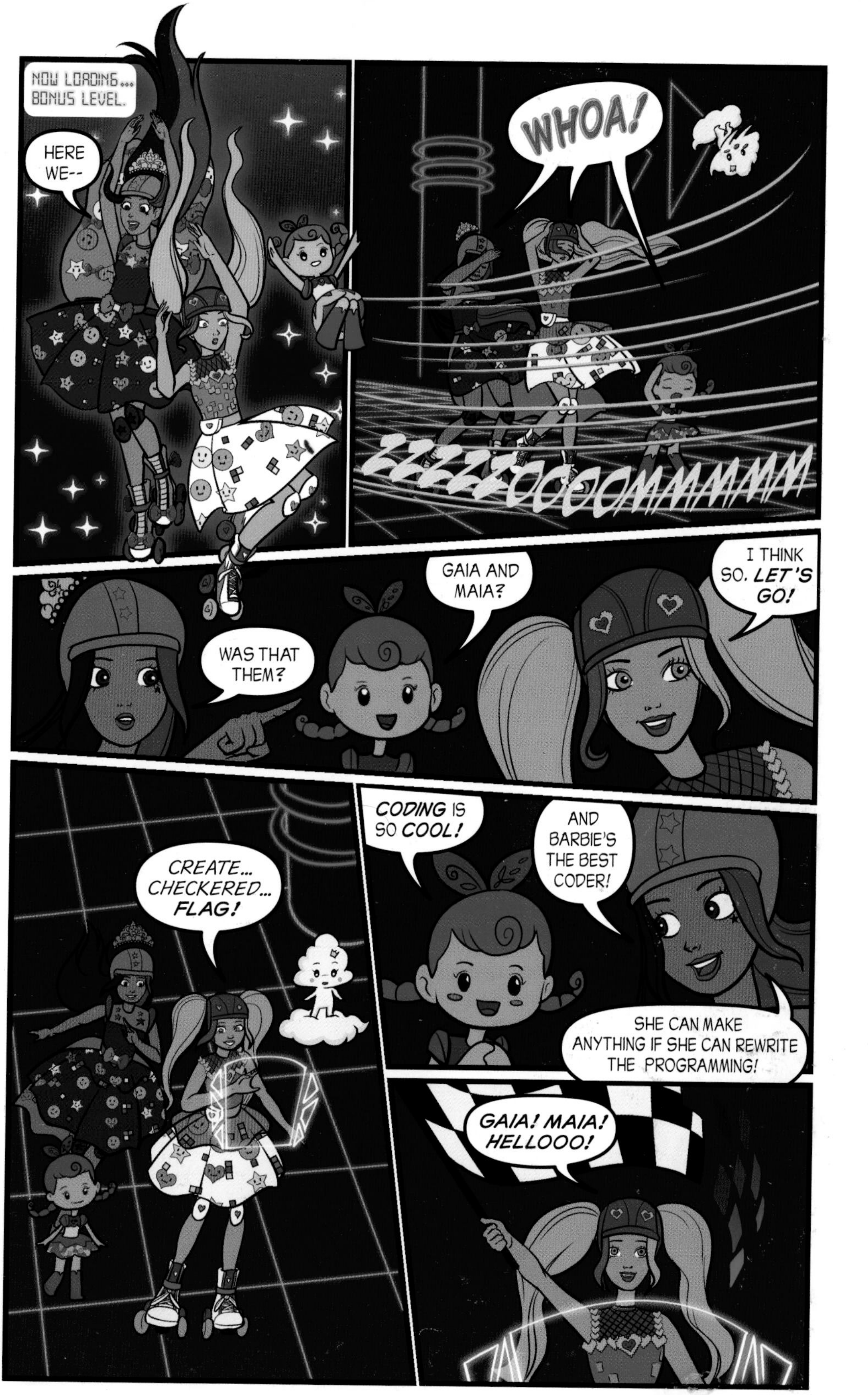
NOW LOADING... BONUS LEVEL.
HERE WE--
WHOA!
ZZZZZOOOOMMMMMM
WAS THAT THEM?
GAIA AND MAIA?
I THINK SO. LET'S GO!
CREATE... CHECKERED... FLAG!
CODING IS SO COOL!
AND BARBIE'S THE BEST CODER!
SHE CAN MAKE ANYTHING IF SHE CAN REWRITE THE PROGRAMMING!
GAIA! MAIA! HELLOOO!

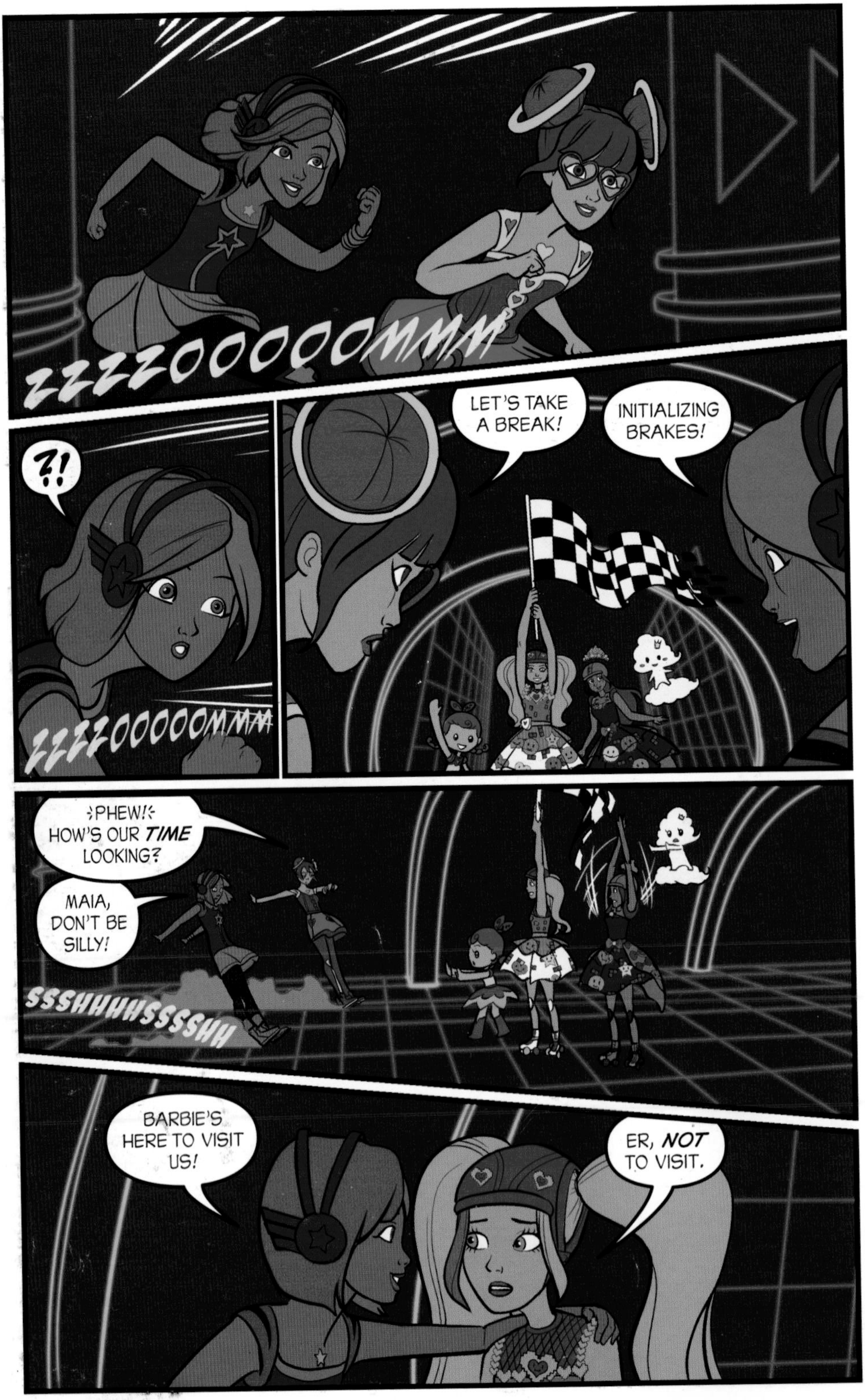
ZZZZOOOOOOMMM
?!
ZZZZOOOOOMMM
LET'S TAKE A BREAK!
INITIALIZING BRAKES!
PHEW! HOW'S OUR TIME LOOKING?
MAIA, DON'T BE SILLY!
SSSHHHHSSSSHH
BARBIE'S HERE TO VISIT US!
ER, NOT TO VISIT.

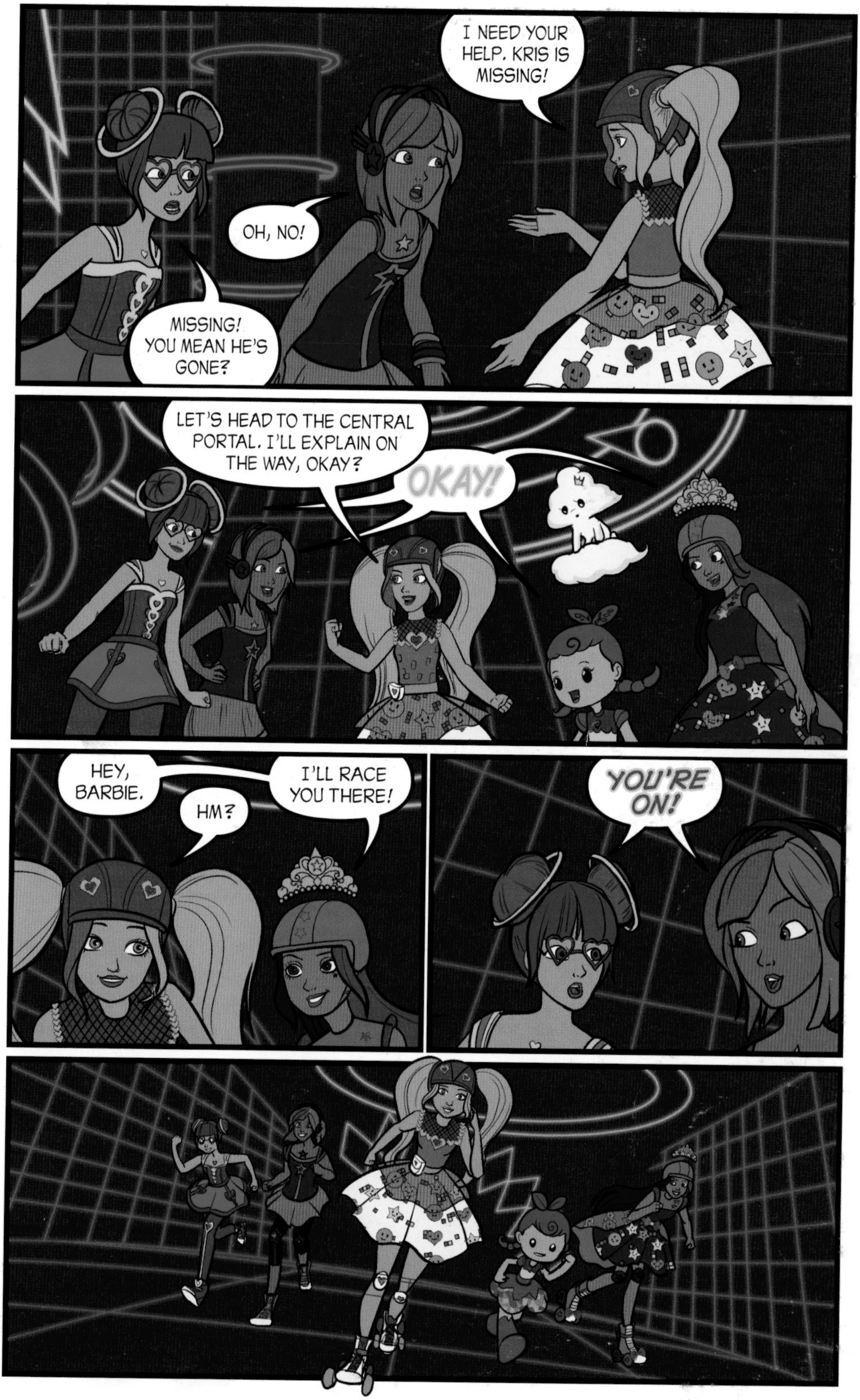
I NEED YOUR HELP. KRIS IS MISSING!
OH, NO!
MISSING! YOU MEAN HE'S GONE?
LET'S HEAD TO THE CENTRAL PORTAL. I'LL EXPLAIN ON THE WAY, OKAY?
OKAY!
HEY, BARBIE.
HM?
I'LL RACE YOU THERE!
YOU'RE ON!

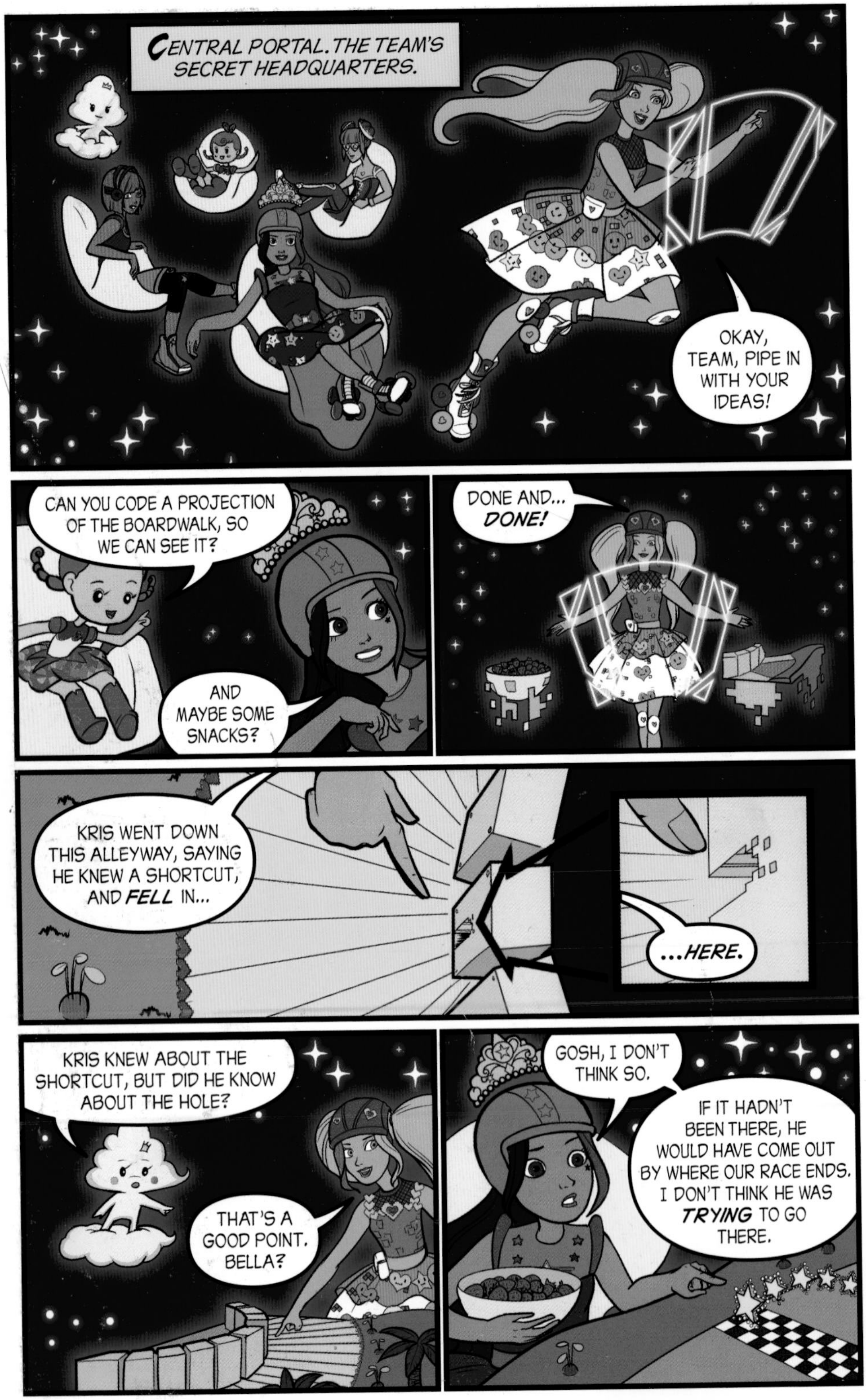
CENTRAL PORTAL. THE TEAM'S SECRET HEADQUARTERS.
OKAY, TEAM, PIPE IN WITH YOUR IDEAS!
CAN YOU CODE A PROJECTION OF THE BOARDWALK, SO WE CAN SEE IT?
AND MAYBE SOME SNACKS?
DONE AND... DONE!
KRIS WENT DOWN THIS ALLEYWAY, SAYING HE KNEW A SHORTCUT, AND FELL IN...
...HERE.
KRIS KNEW ABOUT THE SHORTCUT, BUT DID HE KNOW ABOUT THE HOLE?
THAT'S A GOOD POINT. BELLA?
GOSH, I DON'T THINK SO.
IF IT HADN'T BEEN THERE, HE WOULD HAVE COME OUT BY WHERE OUR RACE ENDS. I DON'T THINK HE WAS TRYING TO GO THERE.

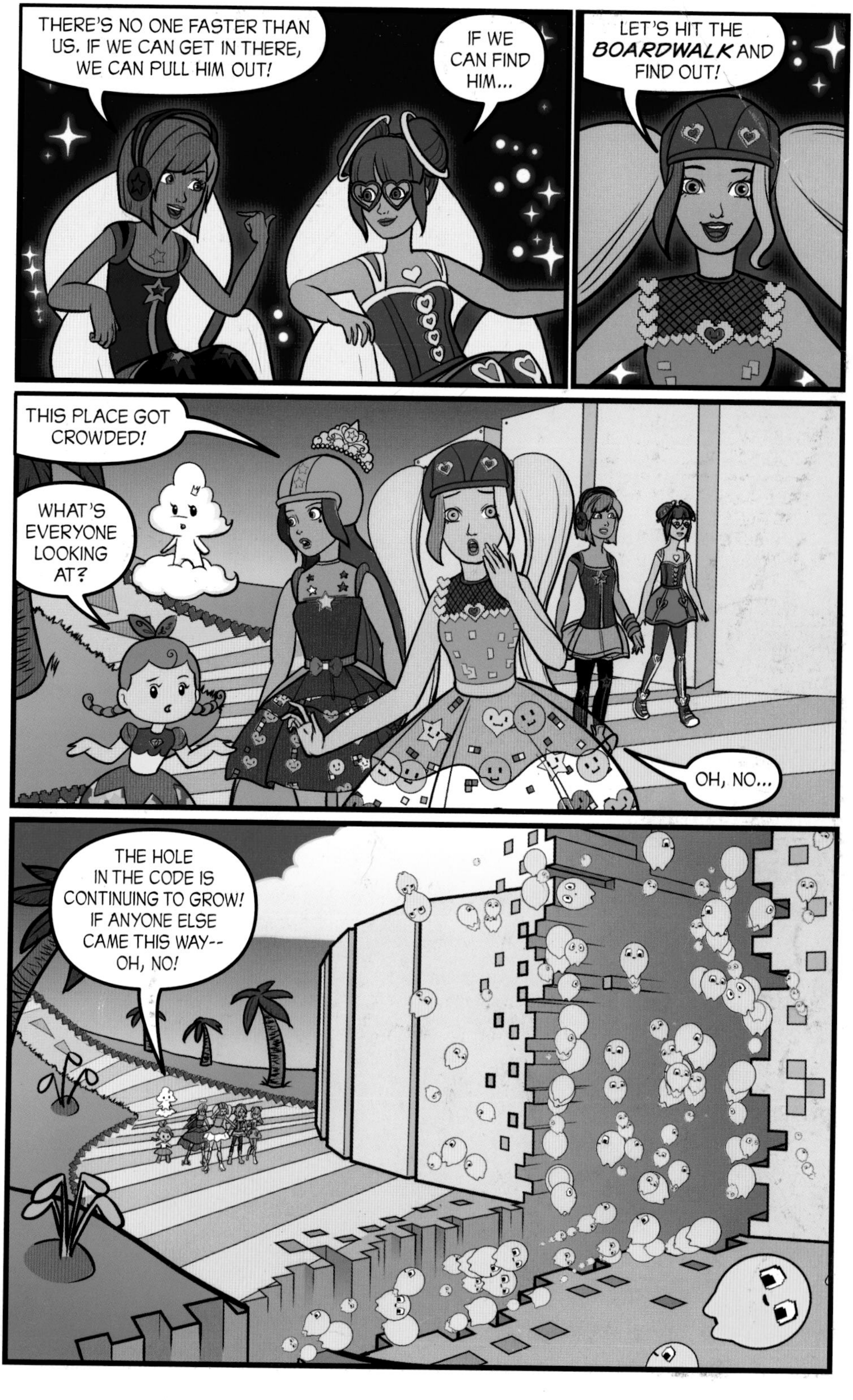
THERE'S NO ONE FASTER THAN US. IF WE CAN GET IN THERE, WE CAN PULL HIM OUT!
IF WE CAN FIND HIM...
LET'S HIT THE *BOARDWALK* AND FIND OUT!
THIS PLACE GOT CROWDED!
WHAT'S EVERYONE LOOKING AT?
OH, NO...
THE HOLE IN THE CODE IS CONTINUING TO GROW! IF ANYONE ELSE CAME THIS WAY-- OH, NO!

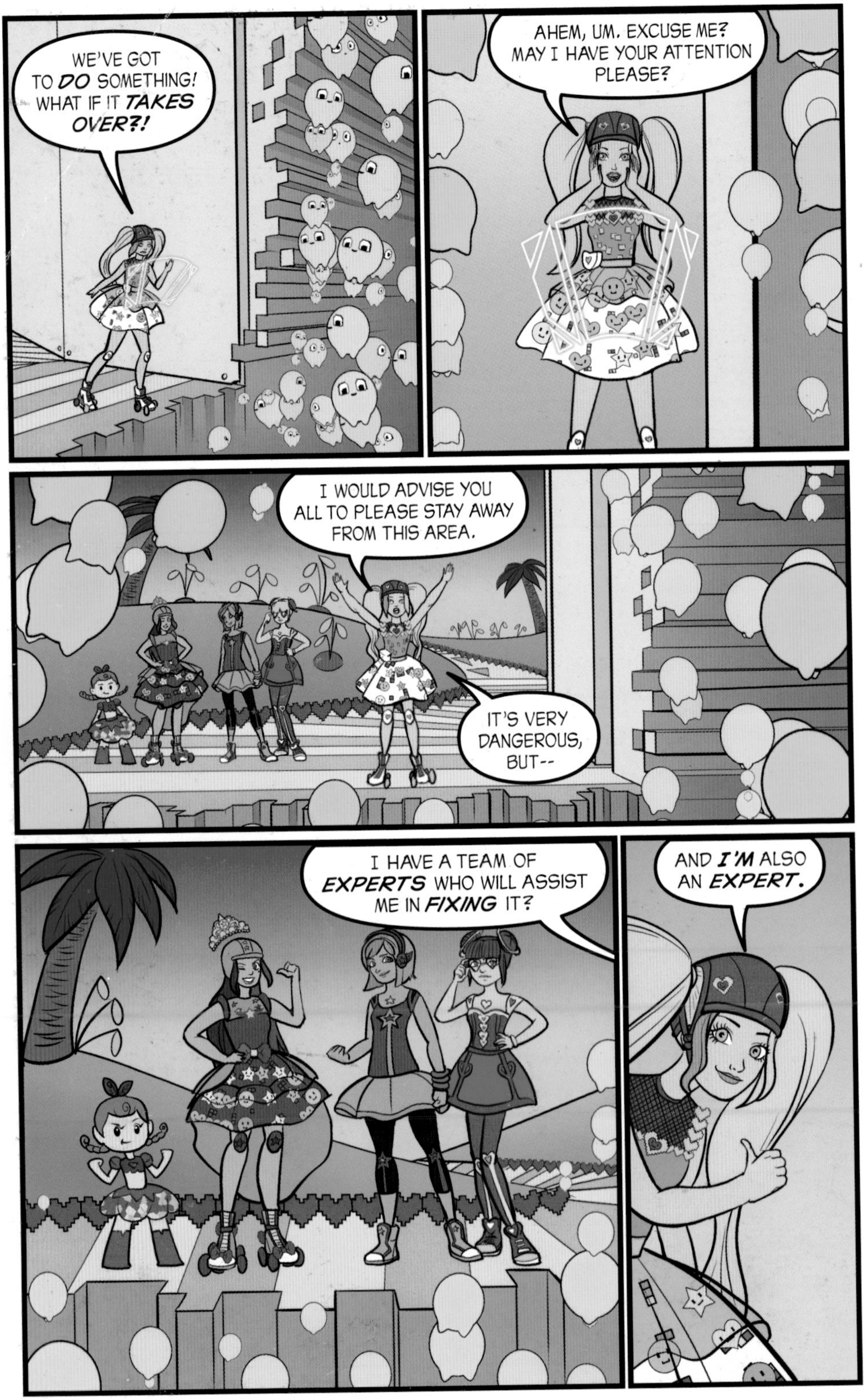
WE'VE GOT TO DO SOMETHING! WHAT IF IT TAKES OVER?!
AHEM, UM. EXCUSE ME? MAY I HAVE YOUR ATTENTION PLEASE?
I WOULD ADVISE YOU ALL TO PLEASE STAY AWAY FROM THIS AREA.
IT'S VERY DANGEROUS, BUT--
I HAVE A TEAM OF EXPERTS WHO WILL ASSIST ME IN FIXING IT?
AND I'M ALSO AN EXPERT.

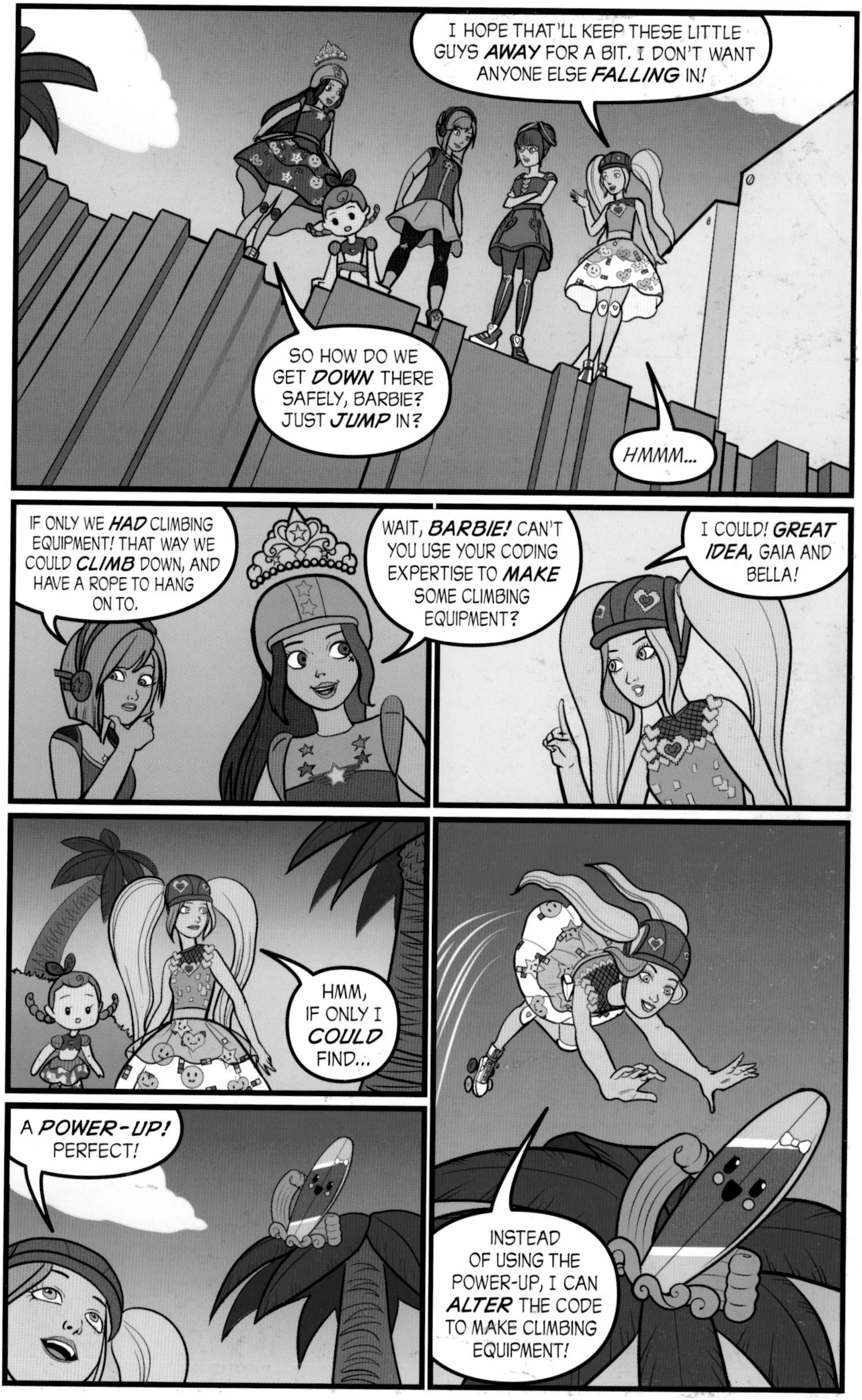
I HOPE THAT'LL KEEP THESE LITTLE GUYS AWAY FOR A BIT. I DON'T WANT ANYONE ELSE FALLING IN!
SO HOW DO WE GET DOWN THERE SAFELY, BARBIE? JUST JUMP IN?
HMMM...
IF ONLY WE HAD CLIMBING EQUIPMENT! THAT WAY WE COULD CLIMB DOWN, AND HAVE A ROPE TO HANG ON TO.
WAIT, BARBIE! CAN'T YOU USE YOUR CODING EXPERTISE TO MAKE SOME CLIMBING EQUIPMENT?
I COULD! GREAT IDEA, GAIA AND BELLA!
HMM, IF ONLY I COULD FIND...
A POWER-UP! PERFECT!
INSTEAD OF USING THE POWER-UP, I CAN ALTER THE CODE TO MAKE CLIMBING EQUIPMENT!

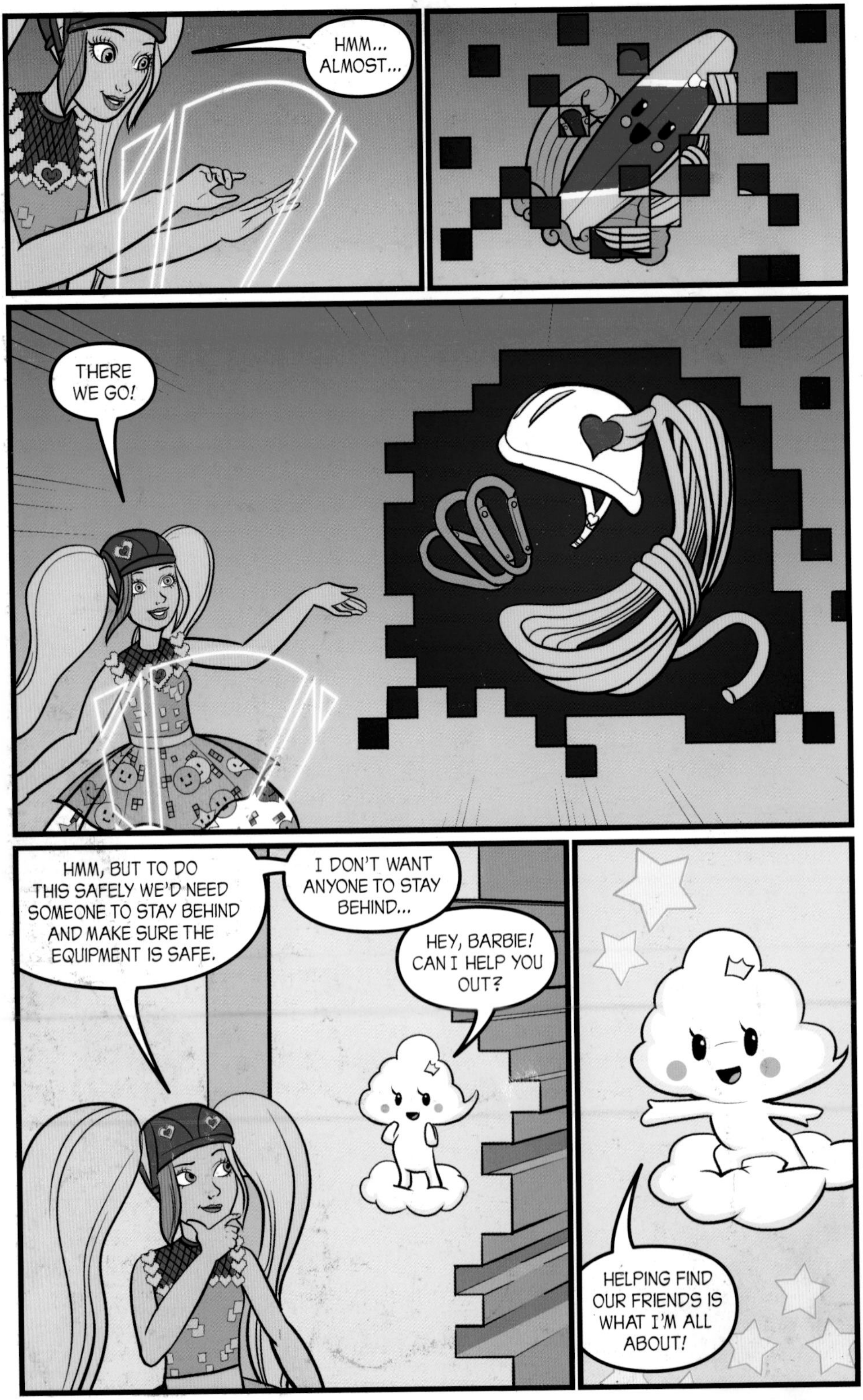
HMM... ALMOST...
THERE WE GO!
HMM, BUT TO DO THIS SAFELY WE'D NEED SOMEONE TO STAY BEHIND AND MAKE SURE THE EQUIPMENT IS SAFE.
I DON'T WANT ANYONE TO STAY BEHIND...
HEY, BARBIE! CAN I HELP YOU OUT?
HELPING FIND OUR FRIENDS IS WHAT I'M ALL ABOUT!

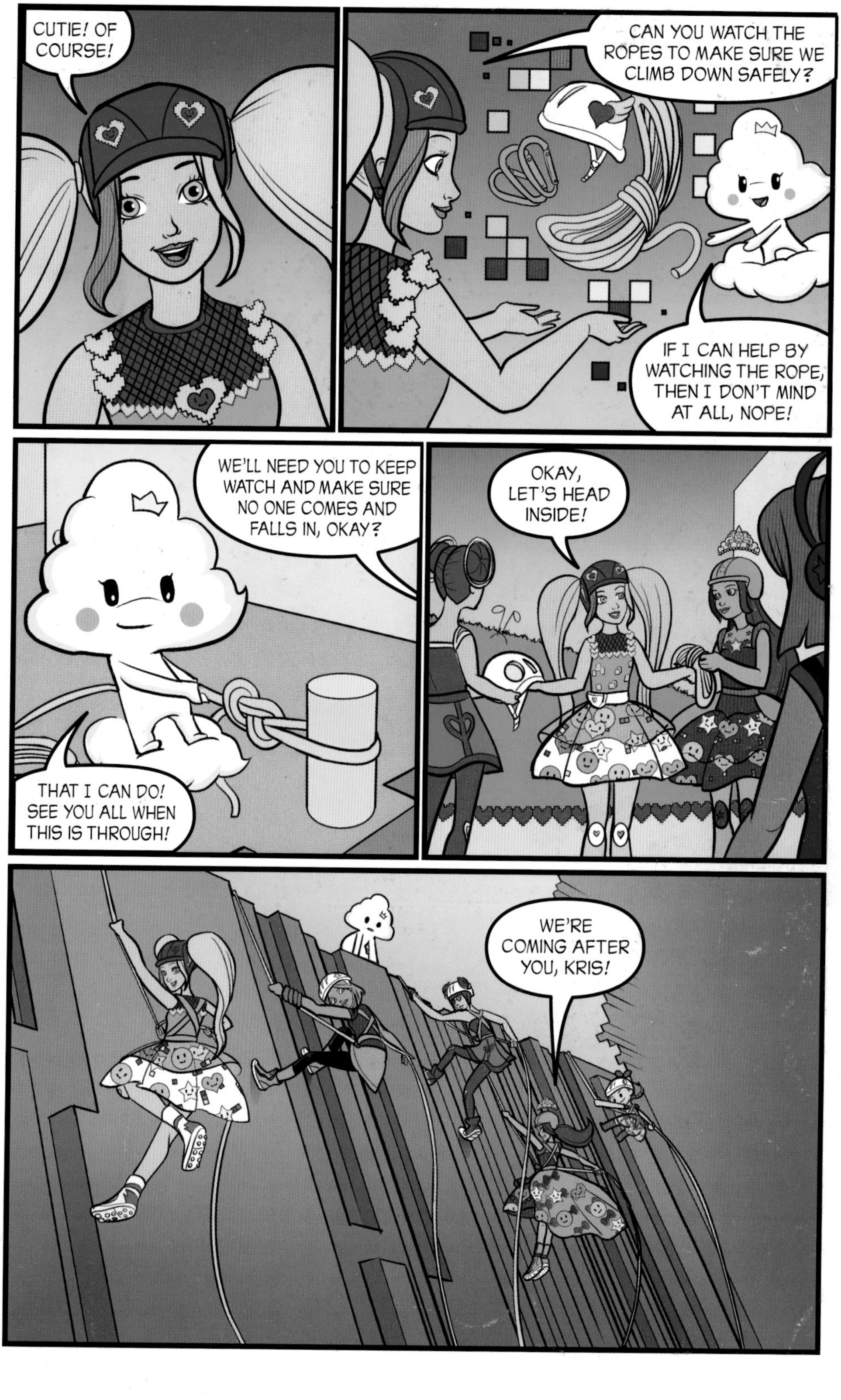
CUTIE! OF COURSE!
CAN YOU WATCH THE ROPES TO MAKE SURE WE CLIMB DOWN SAFELY?
IF I CAN HELP BY WATCHING THE ROPE, THEN I DON'T MIND AT ALL, NOPE!
WE'LL NEED YOU TO KEEP WATCH AND MAKE SURE NO ONE COMES AND FALLS IN, OKAY?
THAT I CAN DO! SEE YOU ALL WHEN THIS IS THROUGH!
OKAY, LET'S HEAD INSIDE!
WE'RE COMING AFTER YOU, KRIS!

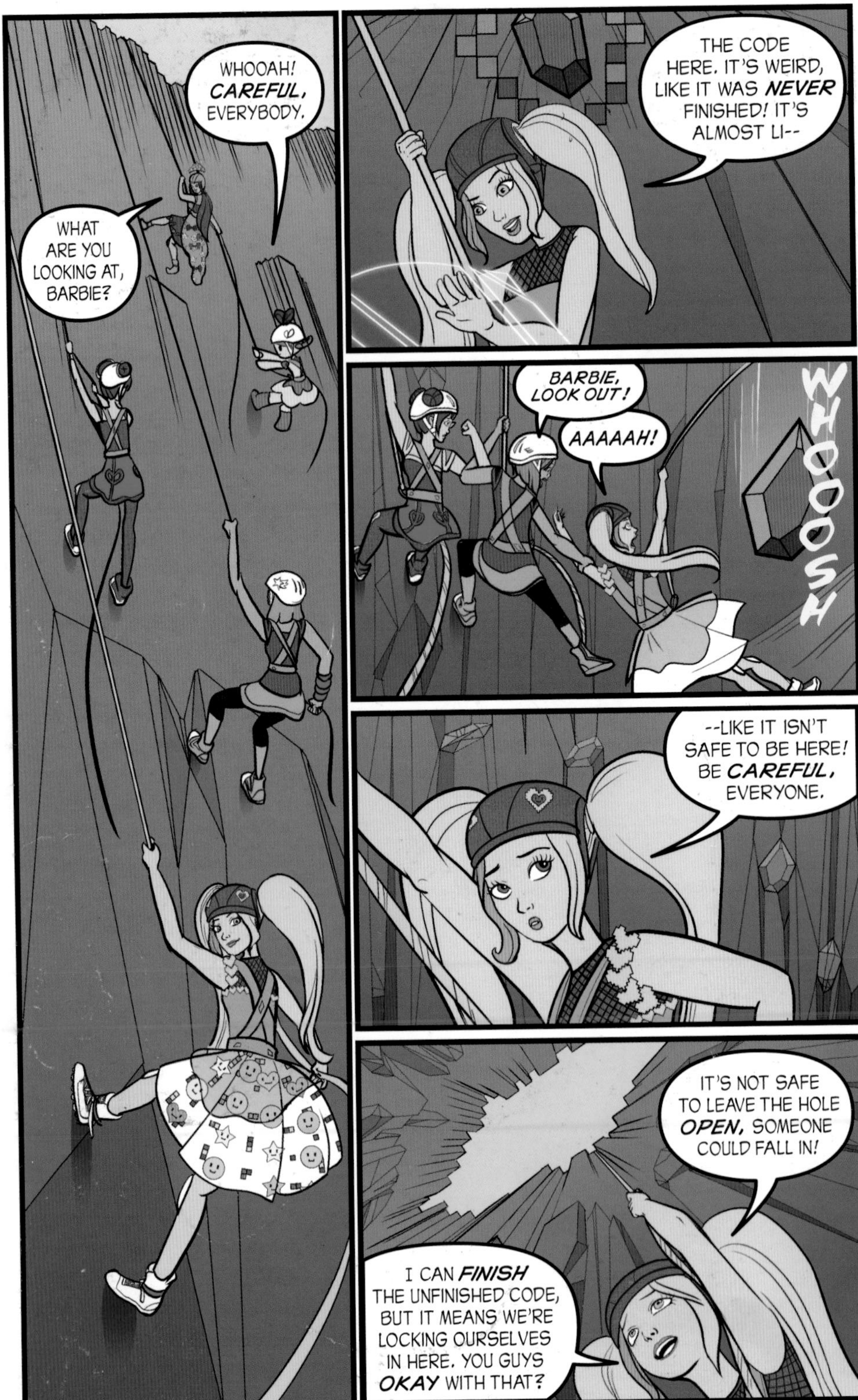
WHOOAH! CAREFUL, EVERYBODY.
WHAT ARE YOU LOOKING AT, BARBIE?
THE CODE HERE. IT'S WEIRD, LIKE IT WAS NEVER FINISHED! IT'S ALMOST LI--
BARBIE, LOOK OUT!
AAAAAH!
WHOOOOSH
--LIKE IT ISN'T SAFE TO BE HERE! BE CAREFUL, EVERYONE.
IT'S NOT SAFE TO LEAVE THE HOLE OPEN, SOMEONE COULD FALL IN!
I CAN FINISH THE UNFINISHED CODE, BUT IT MEANS WE'RE LOCKING OURSELVES IN HERE. YOU GUYS OKAY WITH THAT?

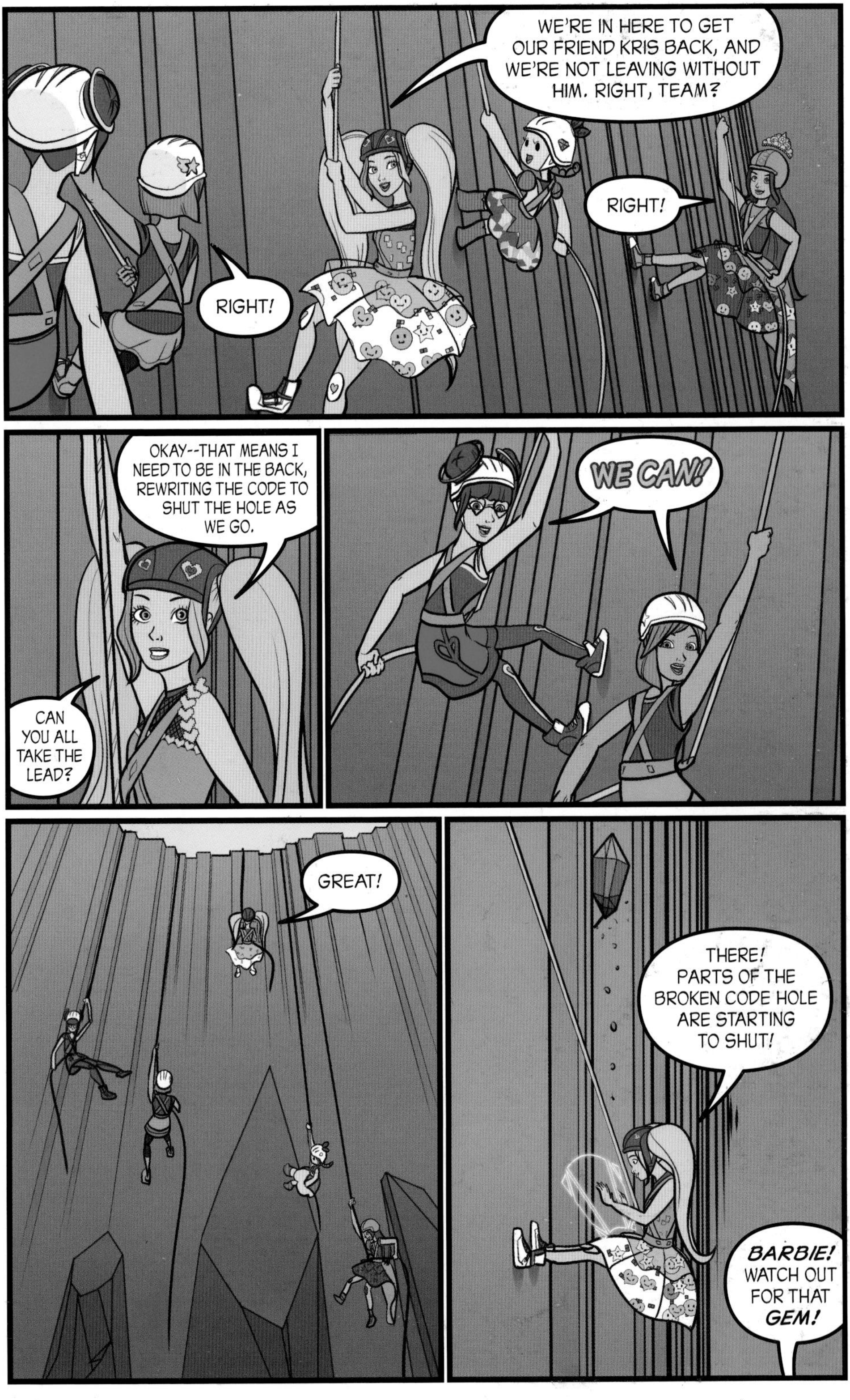
WE'RE IN HERE TO GET OUR FRIEND KRIS BACK, AND WE'RE NOT LEAVING WITHOUT HIM. RIGHT, TEAM?
RIGHT!
RIGHT!
OKAY--THAT MEANS I NEED TO BE IN THE BACK, REWRITING THE CODE TO SHUT THE HOLE AS WE GO.
CAN YOU ALL TAKE THE LEAD?
WE CAN!
GREAT!
THERE! PARTS OF THE BROKEN CODE HOLE ARE STARTING TO SHUT!
BARBIE! WATCH OUT FOR THAT GEM!

GEM?
TRY JELLY INSTEAD!
WHOA!
POWER UP!
NICE!
HERE YOU GO! USE THE SPHERE POWER-UPS TO STOP THE GEM BEFORE THEY GET TO YOU!
BOOP
BOOP
BOOP

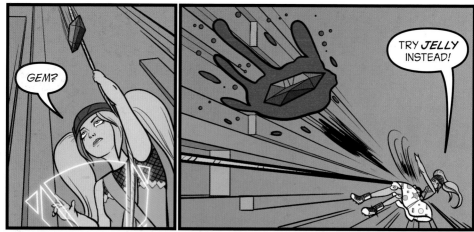

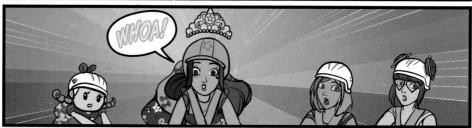

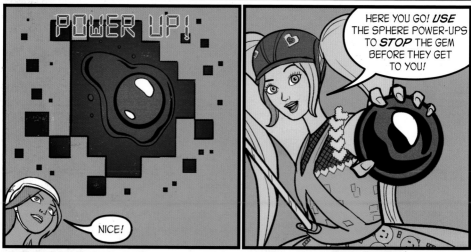

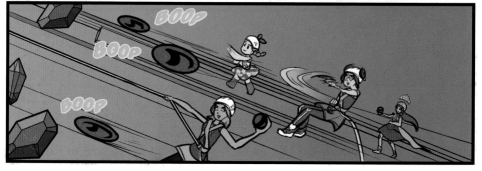

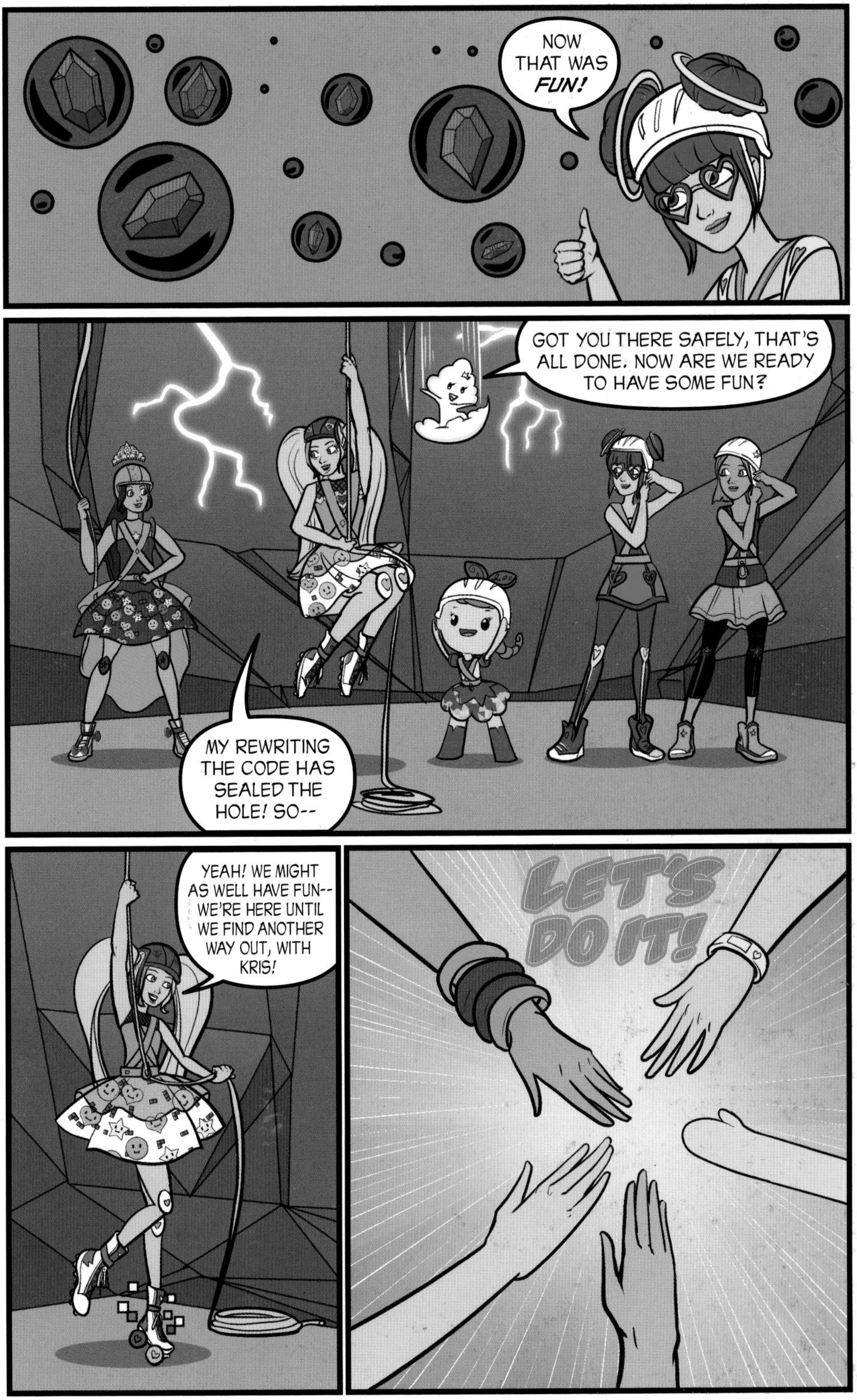
NOW THAT WAS FUN!
GOT YOU THERE SAFELY, THAT'S ALL DONE. NOW ARE WE READY TO HAVE SOME FUN?
MY REWRITING THE CODE HAS SEALED THE HOLE! SO--
YEAH! WE MIGHT AS WELL HAVE FUN-- WE'RE HERE UNTIL WE FIND ANOTHER WAY OUT, WITH KRIS!
LET'S DO IT!

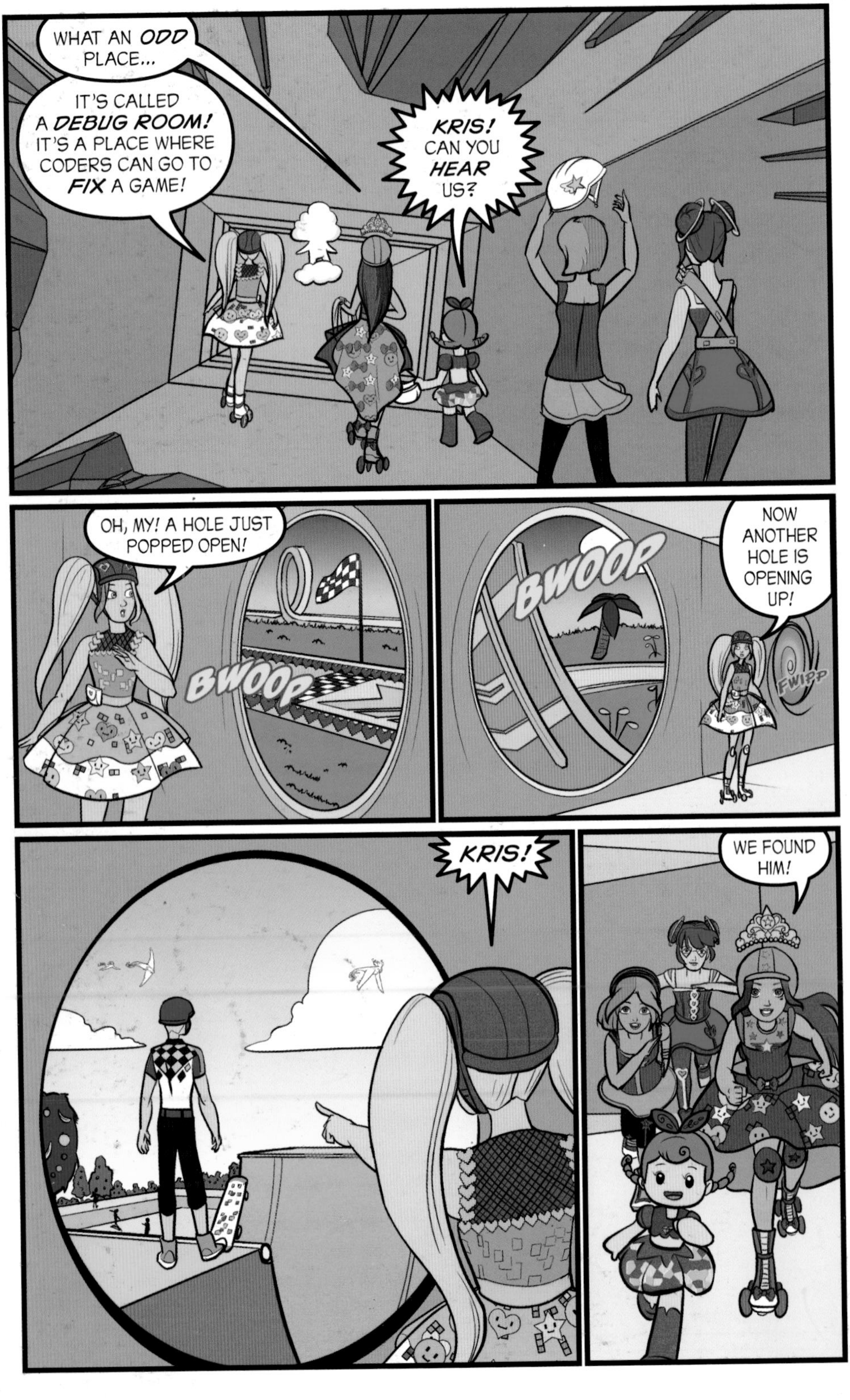
WHAT AN ODD PLACE...
IT'S CALLED A DEBUG ROOM! IT'S A PLACE WHERE CODERS CAN GO TO FIX A GAME!
KRIS! CAN YOU HEAR US?
OH, MY! A HOLE JUST POPPED OPEN!
BWOOP
BWOOP
NOW ANOTHER HOLE IS OPENING UP!
FWIPP
KRIS!
WE FOUND HIM!

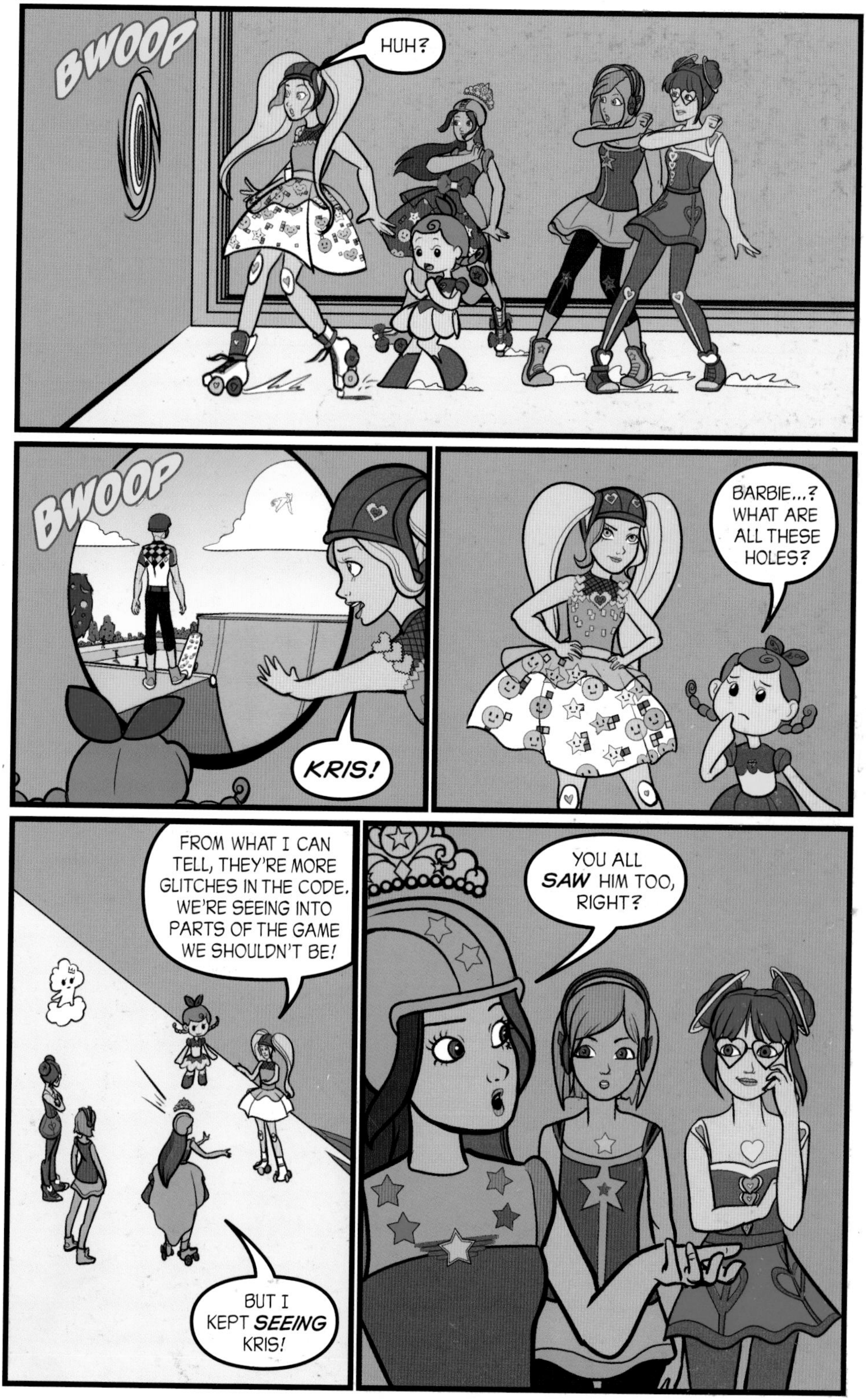
BWOOP
HUH?
BWOOP
KRIS!
BARBIE...? WHAT ARE ALL THESE HOLES?
FROM WHAT I CAN TELL, THEY'RE MORE GLITCHES IN THE CODE. WE'RE SEEING INTO PARTS OF THE GAME WE SHOULDN'T BE!
BUT I KEPT SEEING KRIS!
YOU ALL SAW HIM TOO, RIGHT?

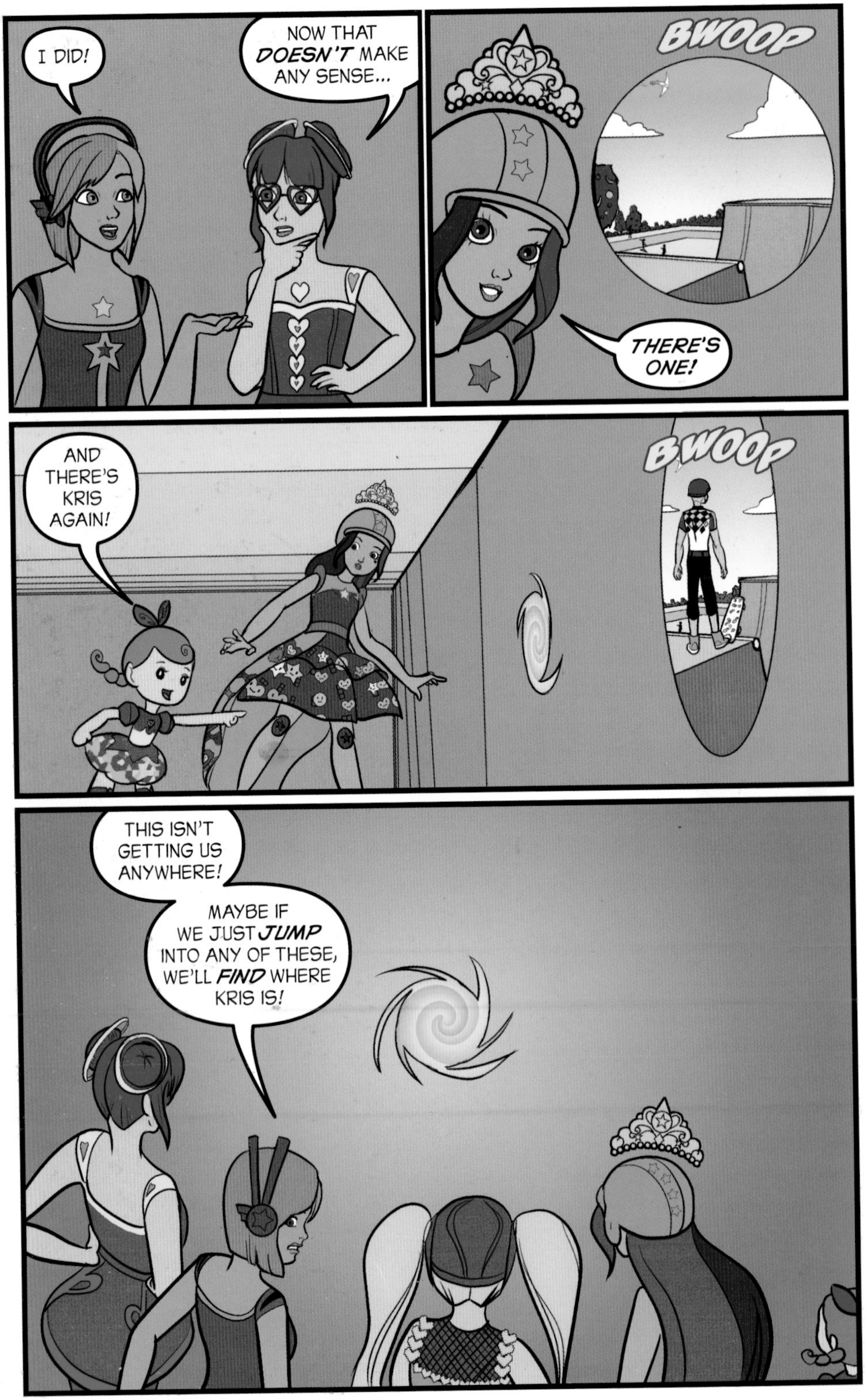
I DID!
NOW THAT DOESN'T MAKE ANY SENSE...
BWOOP
THERE'S ONE!
AND THERE'S KRIS AGAIN!
BWOOP
THIS ISN'T GETTING US ANYWHERE!
MAYBE IF WE JUST JUMP INTO ANY OF THESE, WE'LL FIND WHERE KRIS IS!

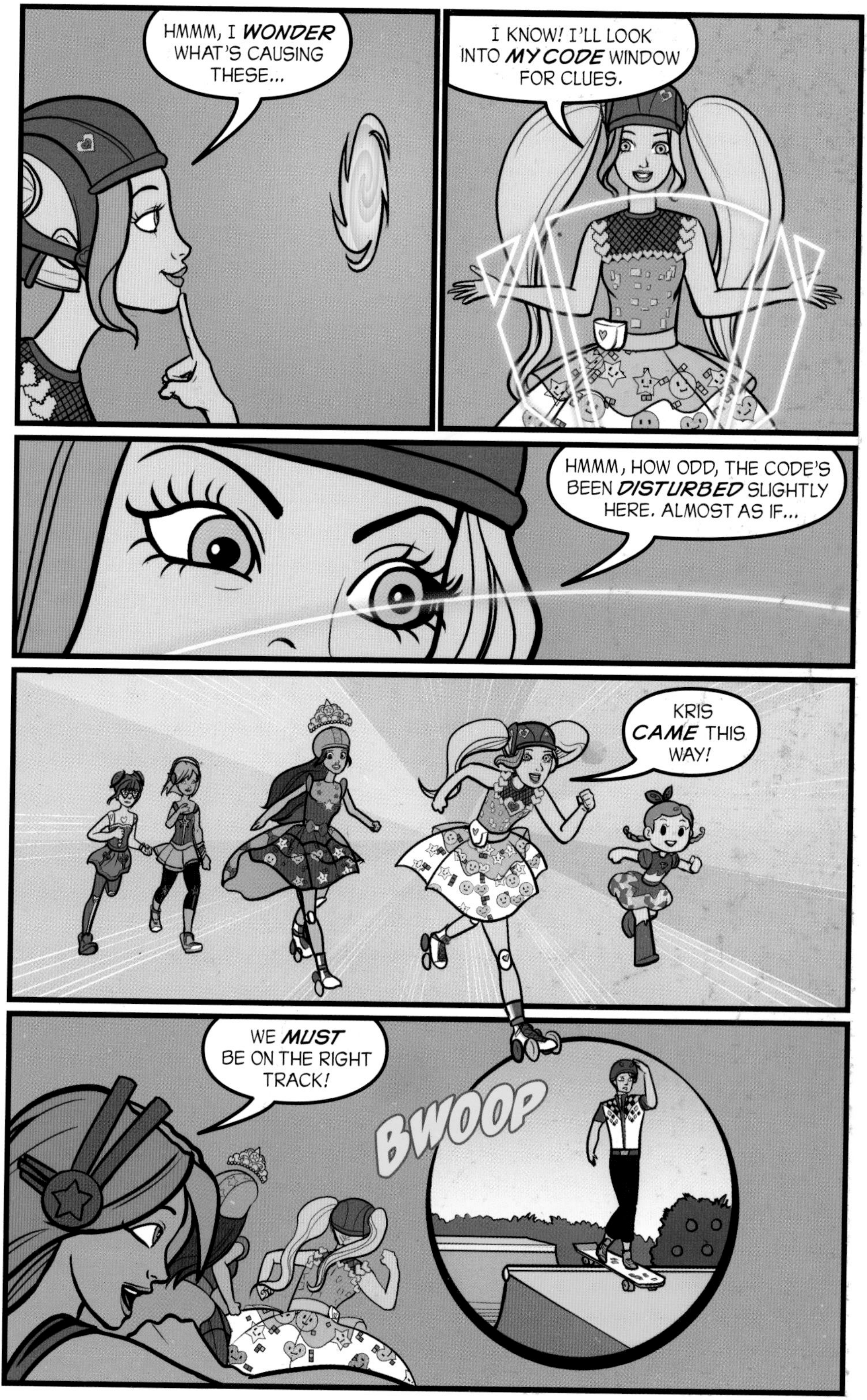
HMMM, I WONDER WHAT'S CAUSING THESE...
I KNOW! I'LL LOOK INTO MY CODE WINDOW FOR CLUES.
HMMM, HOW ODD, THE CODE'S BEEN DISTURBED SLIGHTLY HERE. ALMOST AS IF...
KRIS CAME THIS WAY!
WE MUST BE ON THE RIGHT TRACK!
BWOOP

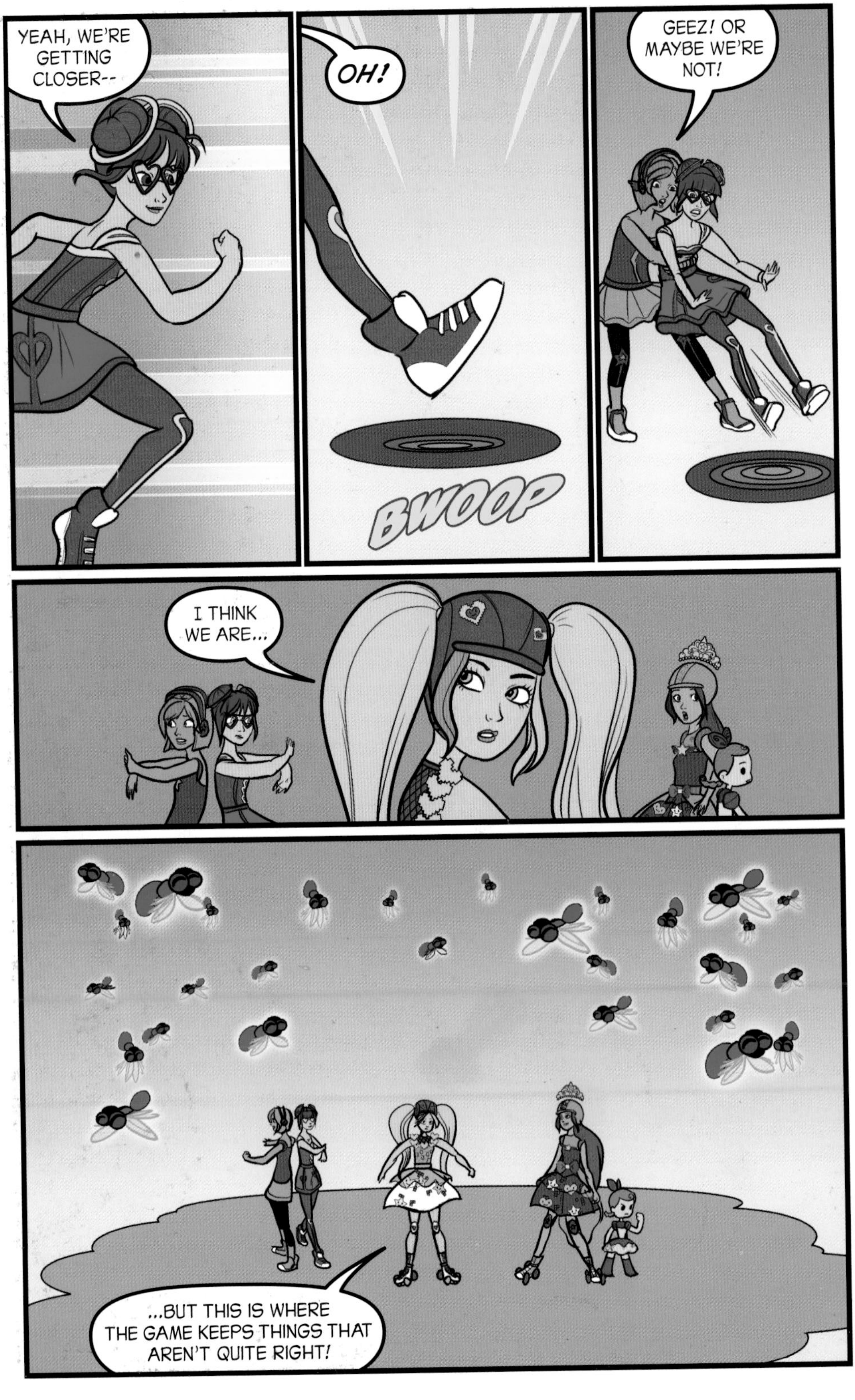
YEAH, WE'RE GETTING CLOSER--
OH!
BWOOP
GEEZ! OR MAYBE WE'RE NOT!
I THINK WE ARE...
...BUT THIS IS WHERE THE GAME KEEPS THINGS THAT AREN'T QUITE RIGHT!

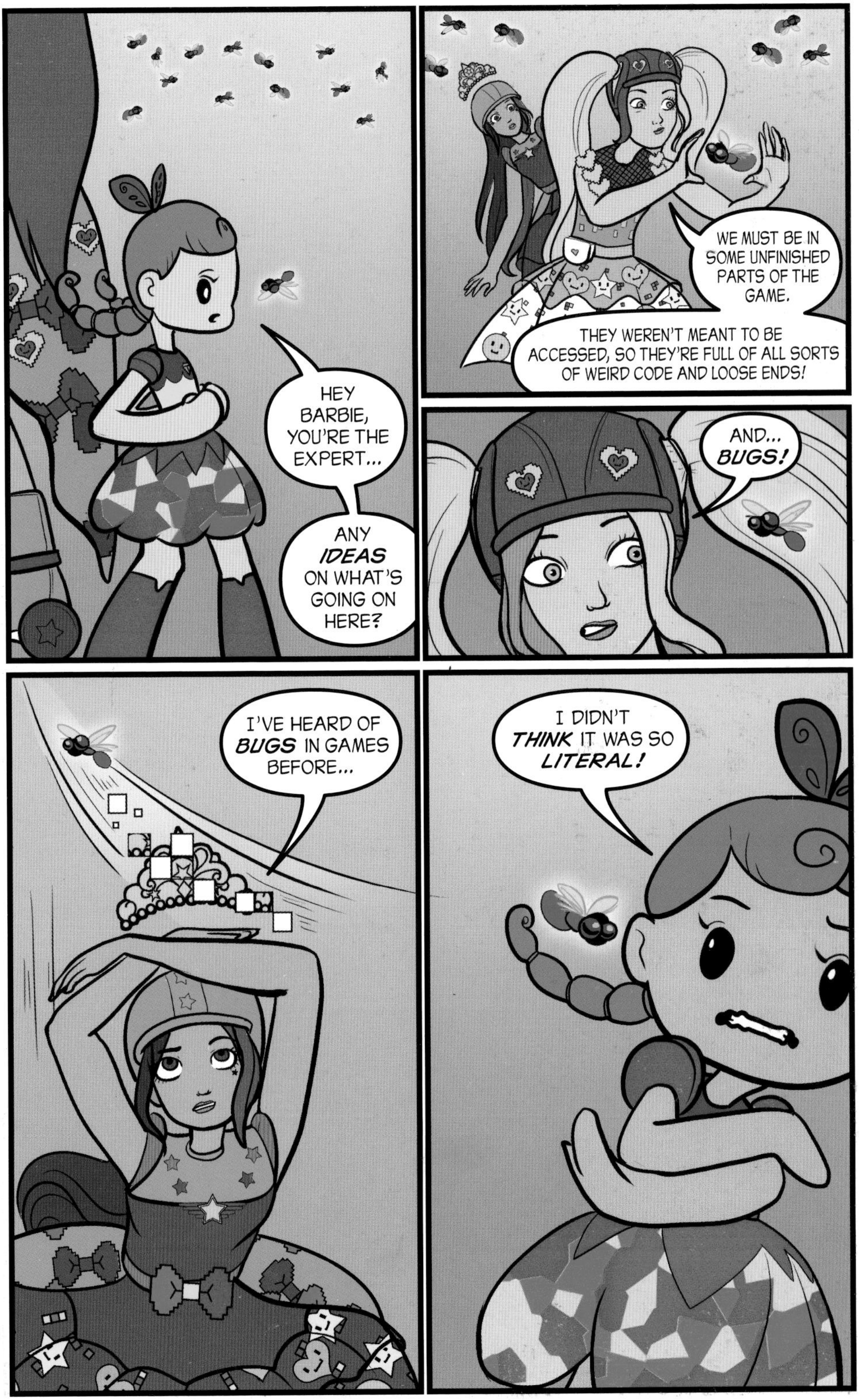

HEY BARBIE, YOU'RE THE EXPERT...
ANY *IDEAS* ON WHAT'S GOING ON HERE?
WE MUST BE IN SOME UNFINISHED PARTS OF THE GAME.
THEY WEREN'T MEANT TO BE ACCESSED, SO THEY'RE FULL OF ALL SORTS OF WEIRD CODE AND LOOSE ENDS!
AND... *BUGS!*
I'VE HEARD OF *BUGS* IN GAMES BEFORE...
I DIDN'T *THINK* IT WAS SO *LITERAL!*

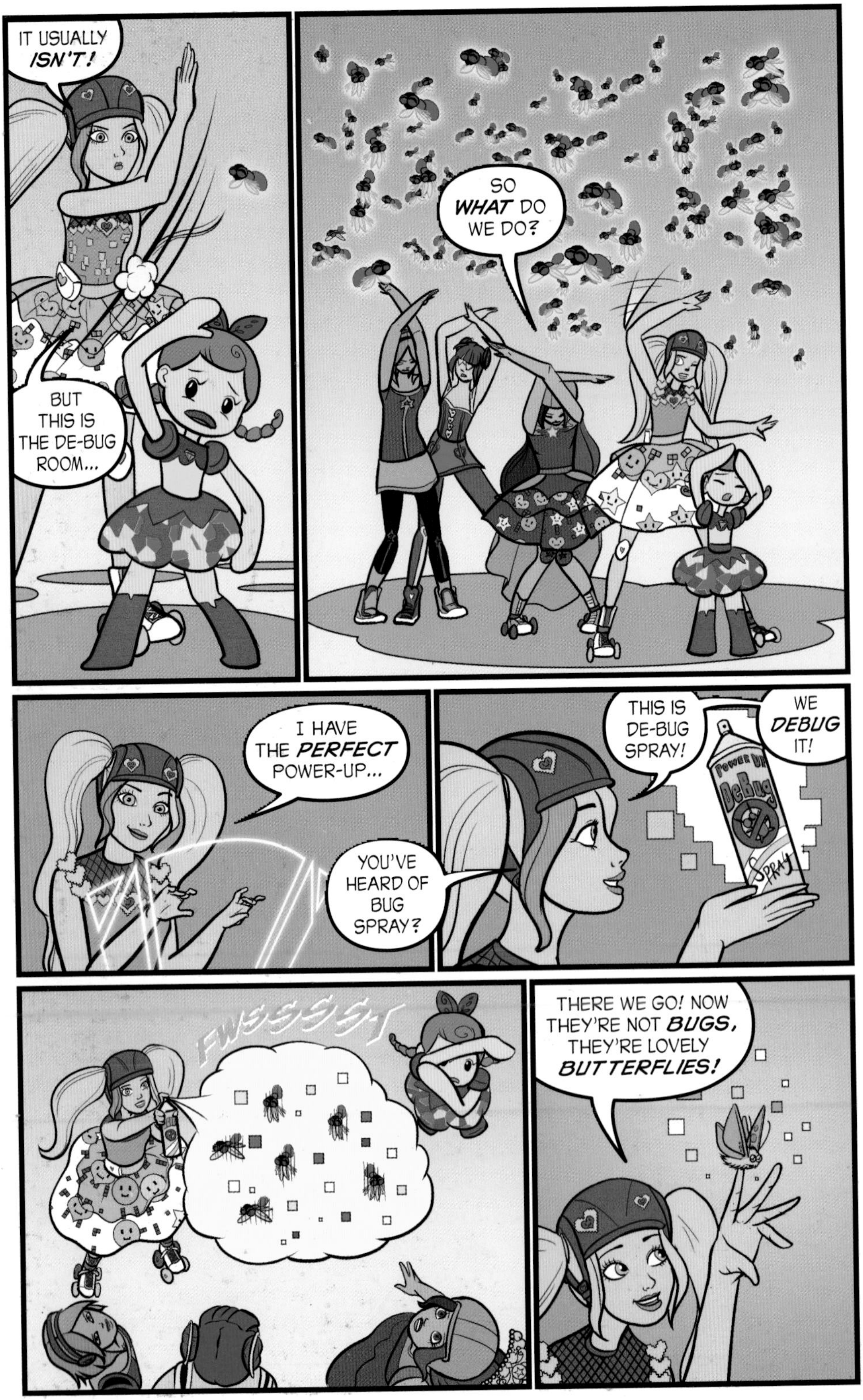

IT USUALLY *ISN'T!*
BUT THIS IS THE DE-BUG ROOM...
SO *WHAT* DO WE DO?
I HAVE THE *PERFECT* POWER-UP...
YOU'VE HEARD OF BUG SPRAY?
THIS IS DE-BUG SPRAY!
WE *DEBUG* IT!
POWER UP DeBug SPRAY
FWSSSST
THERE WE GO! NOW THEY'RE NOT *BUGS,* THEY'RE LOVELY *BUTTERFLIES!*

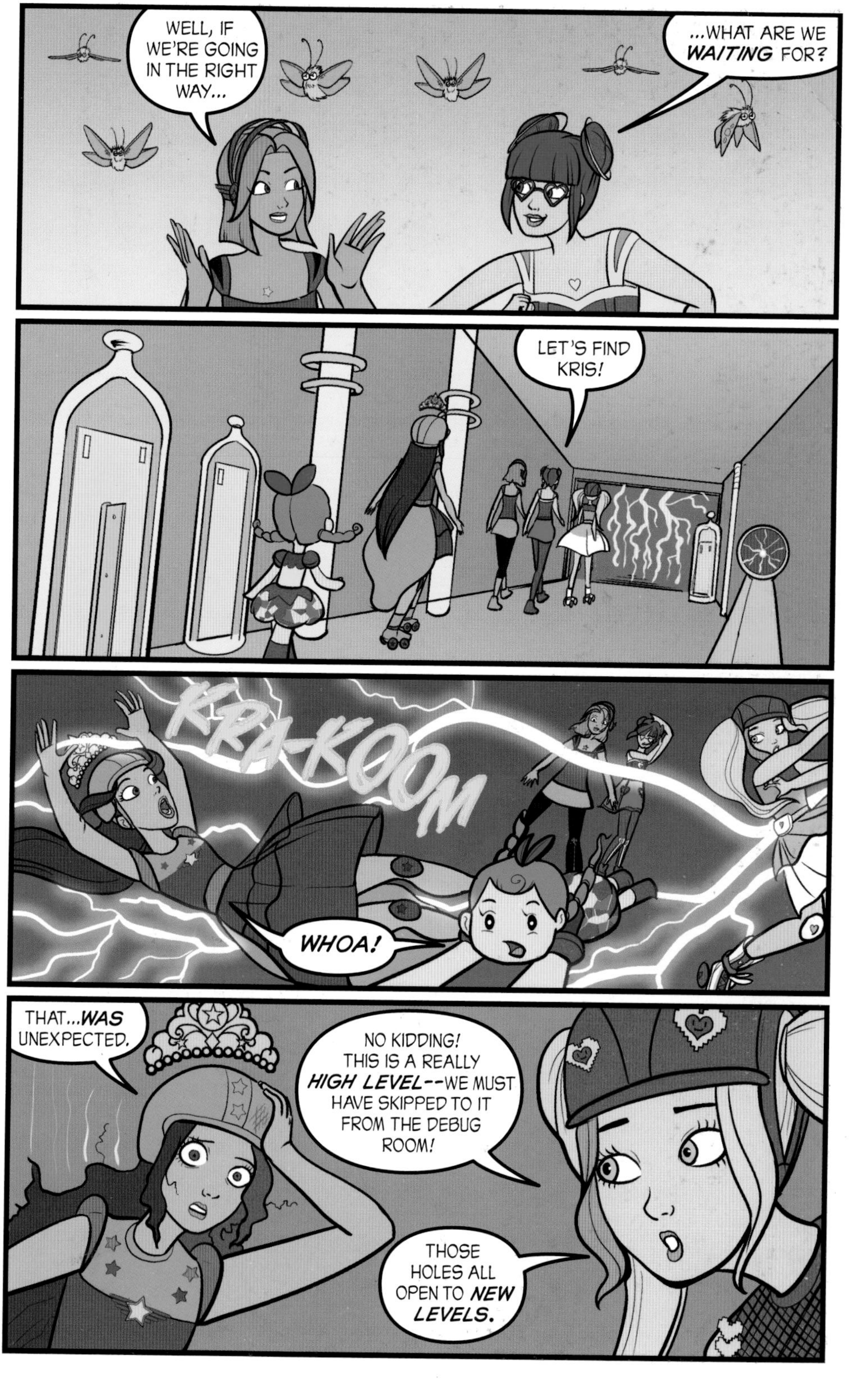
WELL, IF WE'RE GOING IN THE RIGHT WAY...
...WHAT ARE WE *WAITING* FOR?
LET'S FIND KRIS!
KRA-KOOM
WHOA!
THAT...*WAS* UNEXPECTED.
NO KIDDING! THIS IS A REALLY *HIGH LEVEL*--WE MUST HAVE SKIPPED TO IT FROM THE DEBUG ROOM!
THOSE HOLES ALL OPEN TO *NEW LEVELS*.

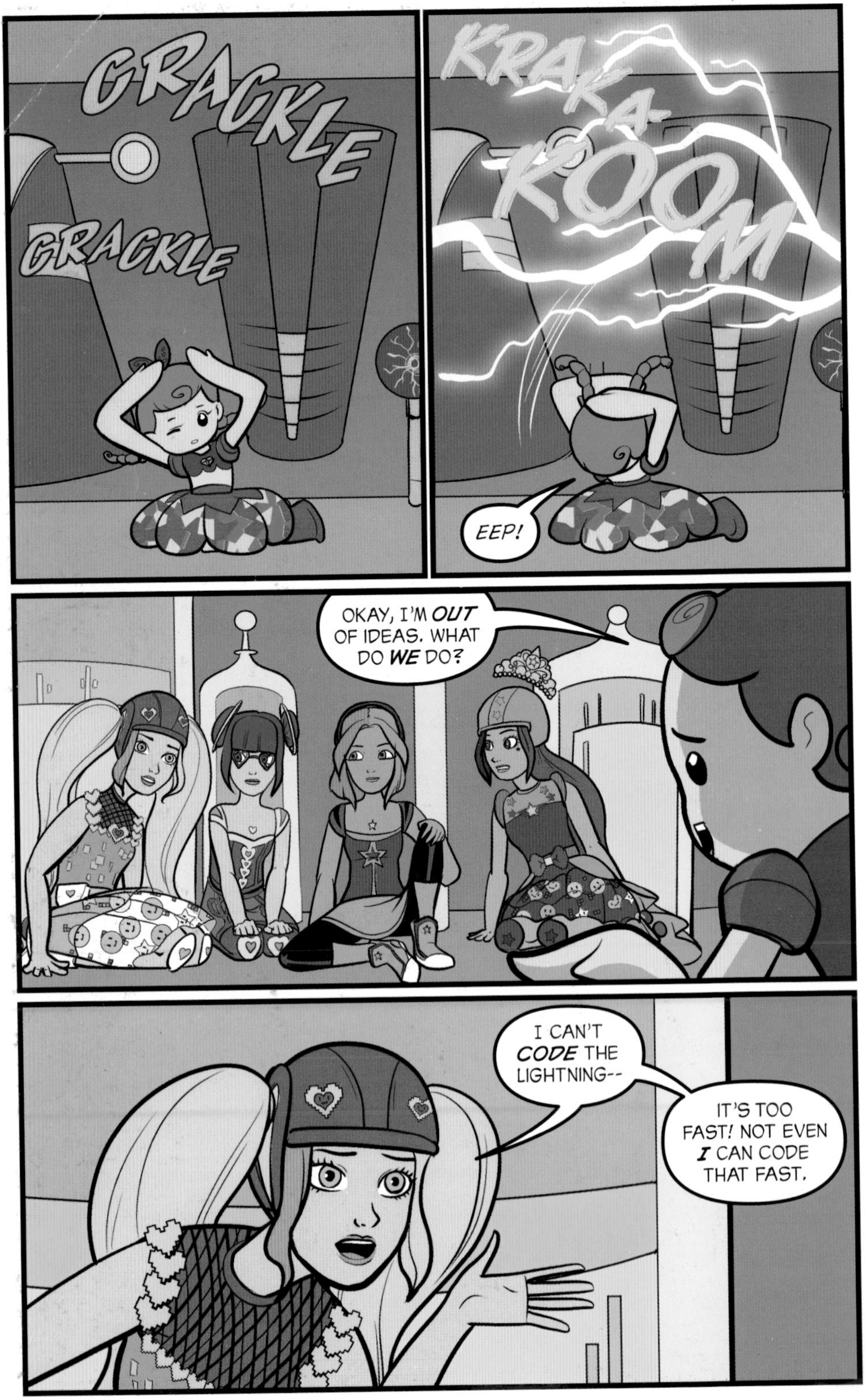
GRACKLE
GRACKLE
KRAKA-KOOM
EEP!
OKAY, I'M OUT OF IDEAS. WHAT DO WE DO?
I CAN'T CODE THE LIGHTNING--
IT'S TOO FAST! NOT EVEN I CAN CODE THAT FAST.

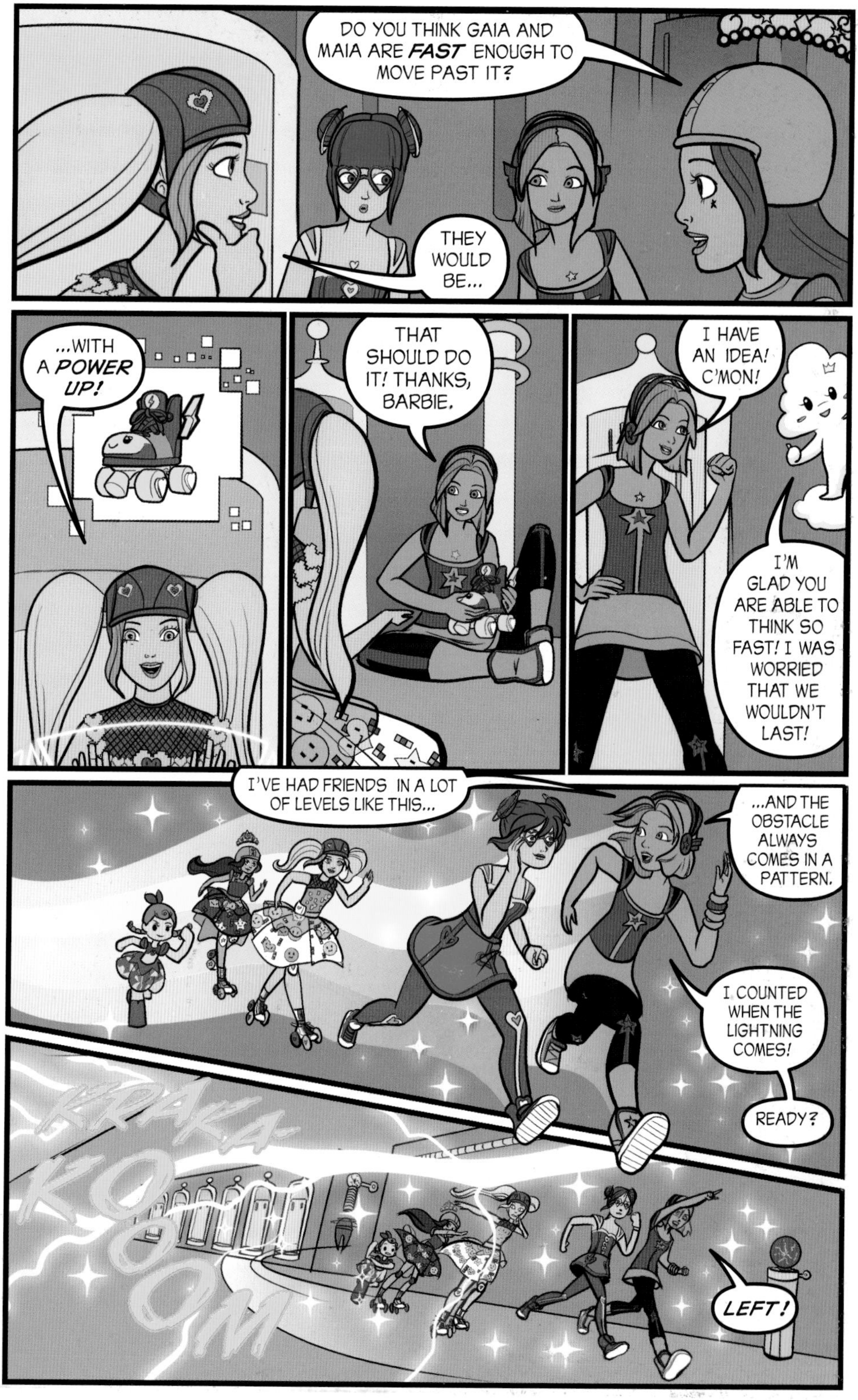
DO YOU THINK GAIA AND MAIA ARE *FAST* ENOUGH TO MOVE PAST IT?
THEY WOULD BE...
...WITH A *POWER UP!*
THAT SHOULD DO IT! THANKS, BARBIE.
I HAVE AN IDEA! C'MON!
I'M GLAD YOU ARE ABLE TO THINK SO FAST! I WAS WORRIED THAT WE WOULDN'T LAST!
I'VE HAD FRIENDS IN A LOT OF LEVELS LIKE THIS...
...AND THE OBSTACLE ALWAYS COMES IN A PATTERN.
I COUNTED WHEN THE LIGHTNING COMES!
READY?
KRAKA-KOOOM
*LEFT!*

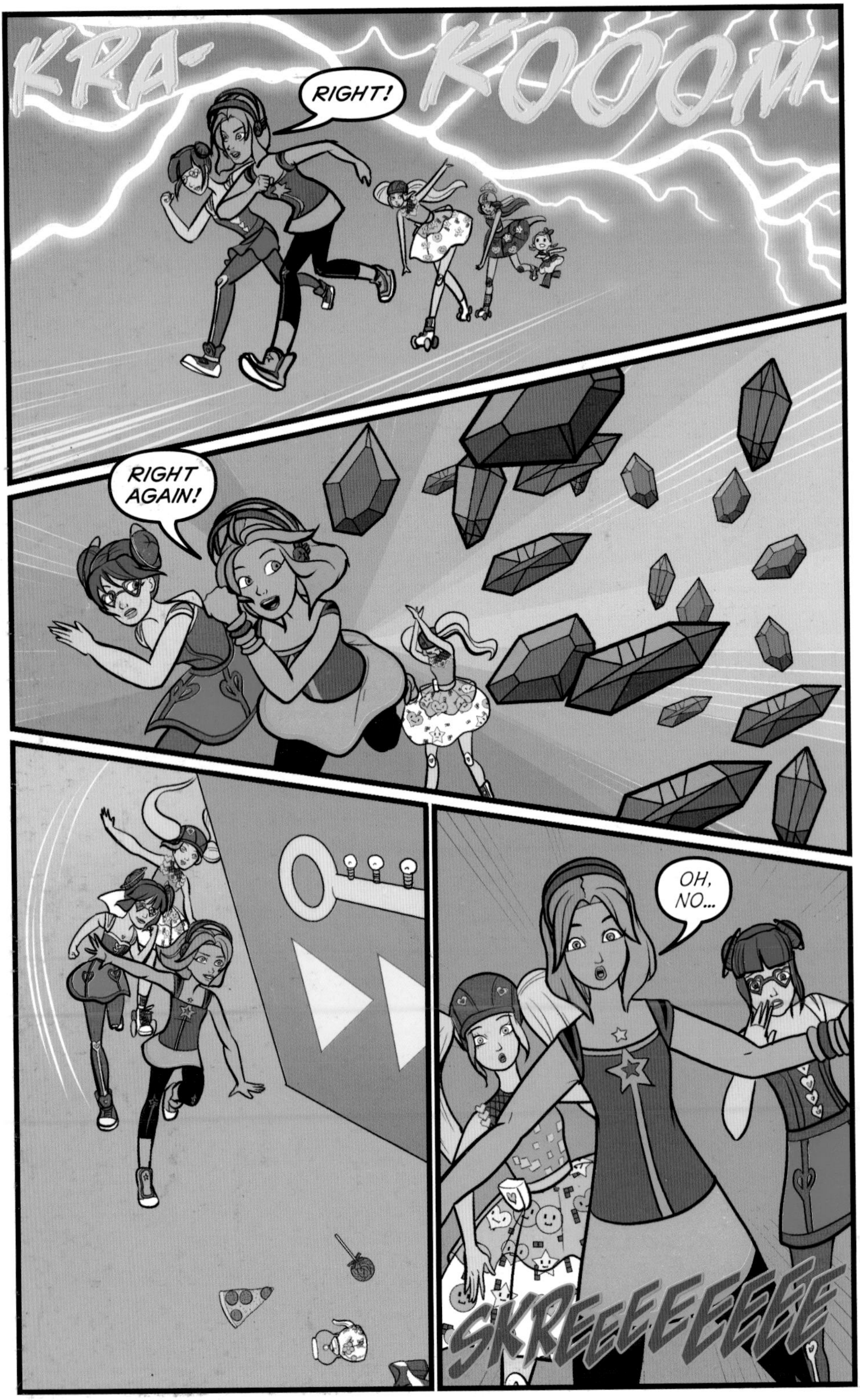
KRA-
KOOOM
RIGHT!
RIGHT AGAIN!
OH, NO...
SKREEEEEEEE

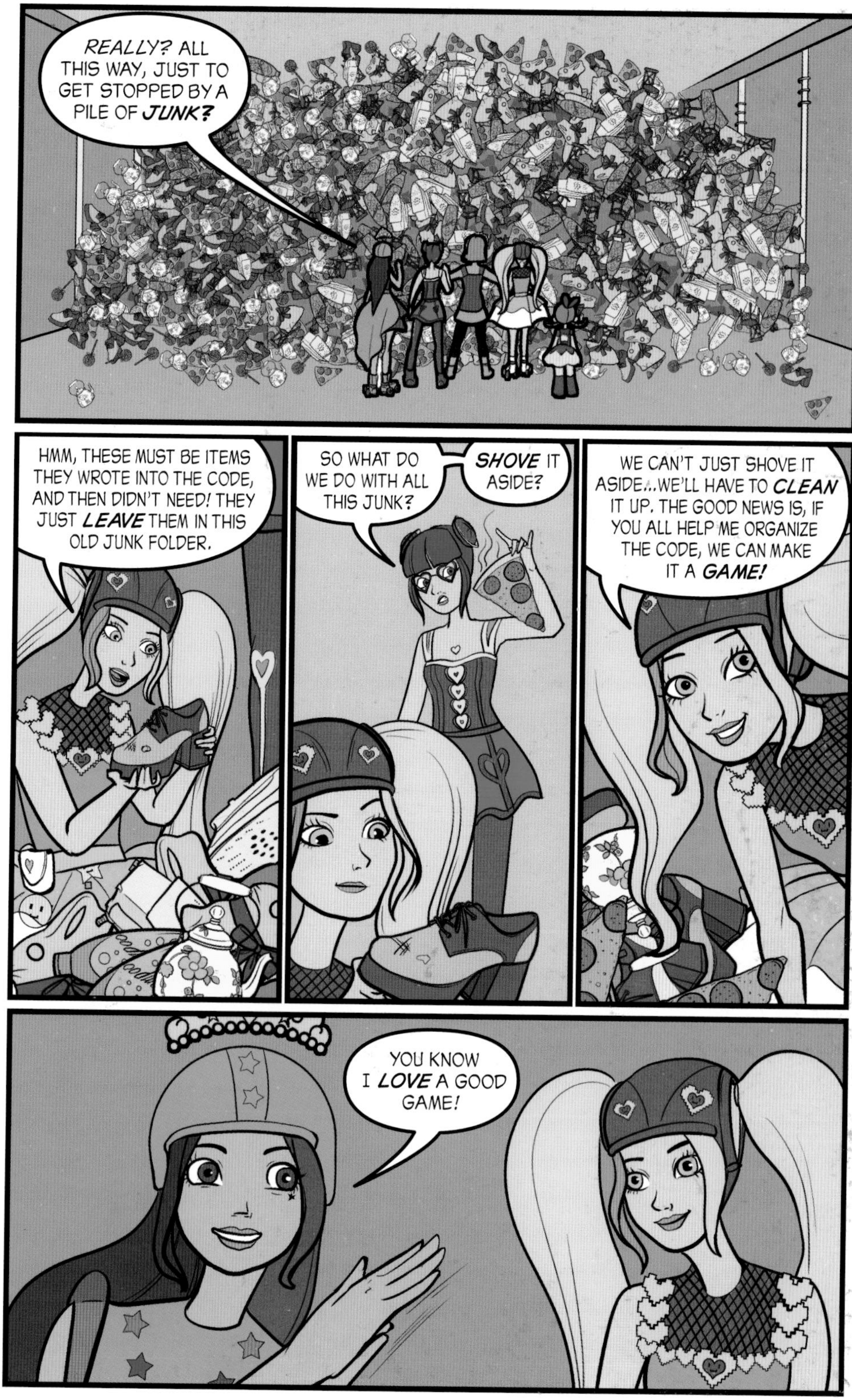

REALLY? ALL THIS WAY, JUST TO GET STOPPED BY A PILE OF JUNK?
HMM, THESE MUST BE ITEMS THEY WROTE INTO THE CODE, AND THEN DIDN'T NEED! THEY JUST LEAVE THEM IN THIS OLD JUNK FOLDER.
SO WHAT DO WE DO WITH ALL THIS JUNK?
SHOVE IT ASIDE?
WE CAN'T JUST SHOVE IT ASIDE...WE'LL HAVE TO CLEAN IT UP. THE GOOD NEWS IS, IF YOU ALL HELP ME ORGANIZE THE CODE, WE CAN MAKE IT A GAME!
YOU KNOW I LOVE A GOOD GAME!

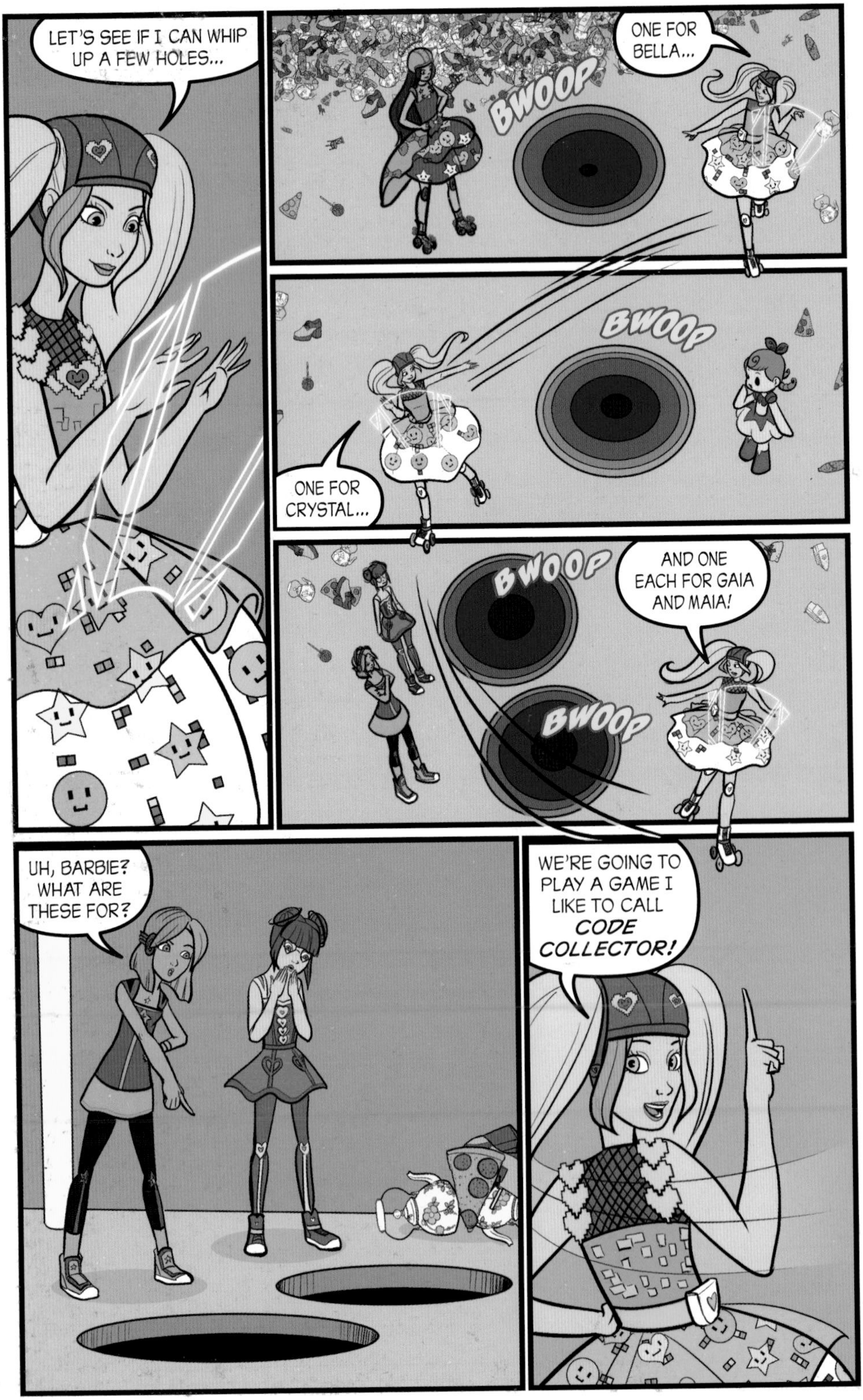
LET'S SEE IF I CAN WHIP UP A FEW HOLES...
ONE FOR BELLA...
BWOOP
BWOOP
ONE FOR CRYSTAL...
BWOOP
AND ONE EACH FOR GAIA AND MAIA!
BWOOP
UH, BARBIE? WHAT ARE THESE FOR?
WE'RE GOING TO PLAY A GAME I LIKE TO CALL *CODE COLLECTOR!*

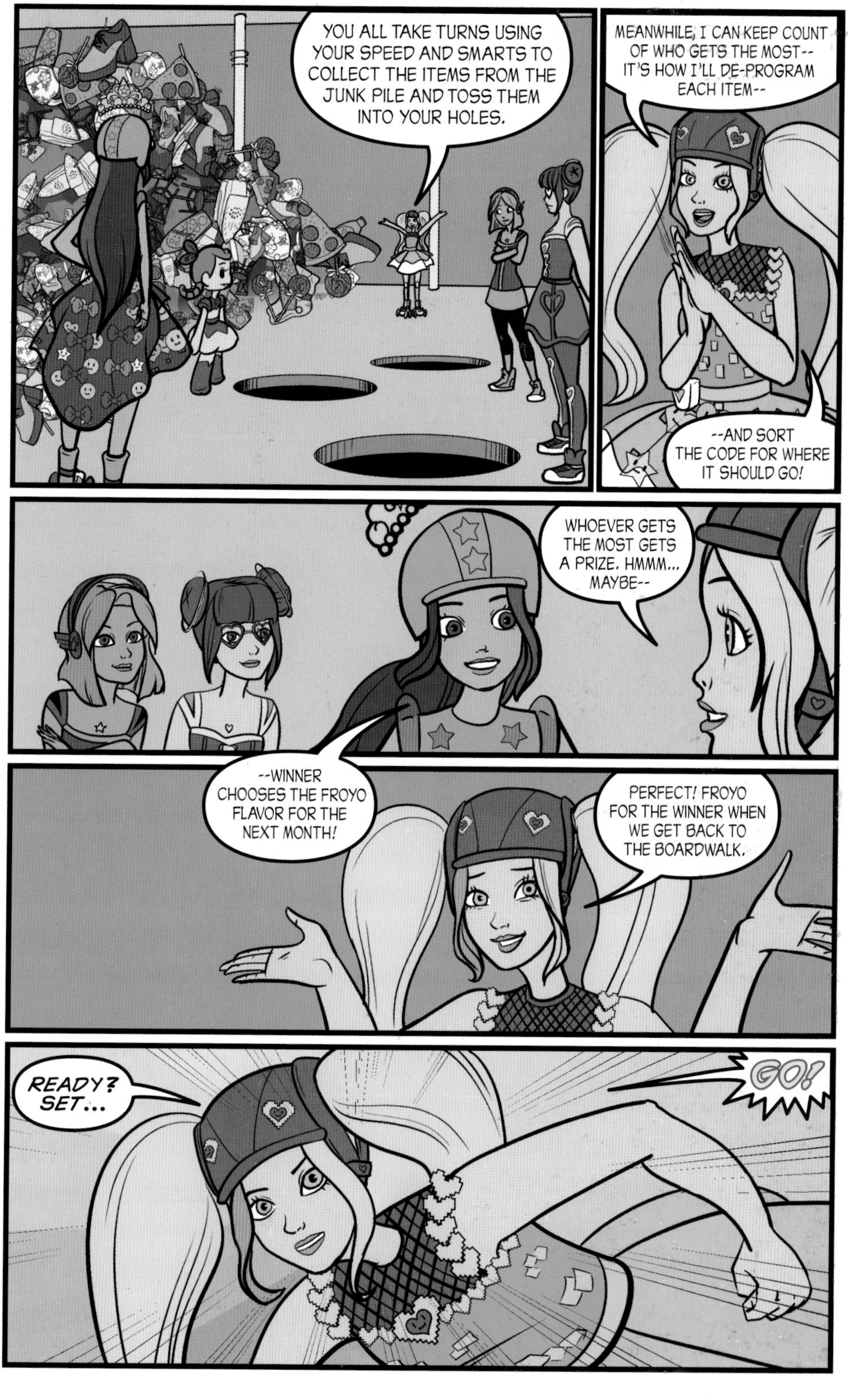
YOU ALL TAKE TURNS USING YOUR SPEED AND SMARTS TO COLLECT THE ITEMS FROM THE JUNK PILE AND TOSS THEM INTO YOUR HOLES.
MEANWHILE, I CAN KEEP COUNT OF WHO GETS THE MOST-- IT'S HOW I'LL DE-PROGRAM EACH ITEM--
--AND SORT THE CODE FOR WHERE IT SHOULD GO!
WHOEVER GETS THE MOST GETS A PRIZE. HMMM... MAYBE--
--WINNER CHOOSES THE FROYO FLAVOR FOR THE NEXT MONTH!
PERFECT! FROYO FOR THE WINNER WHEN WE GET BACK TO THE BOARDWALK.
READY? SET...
GO!

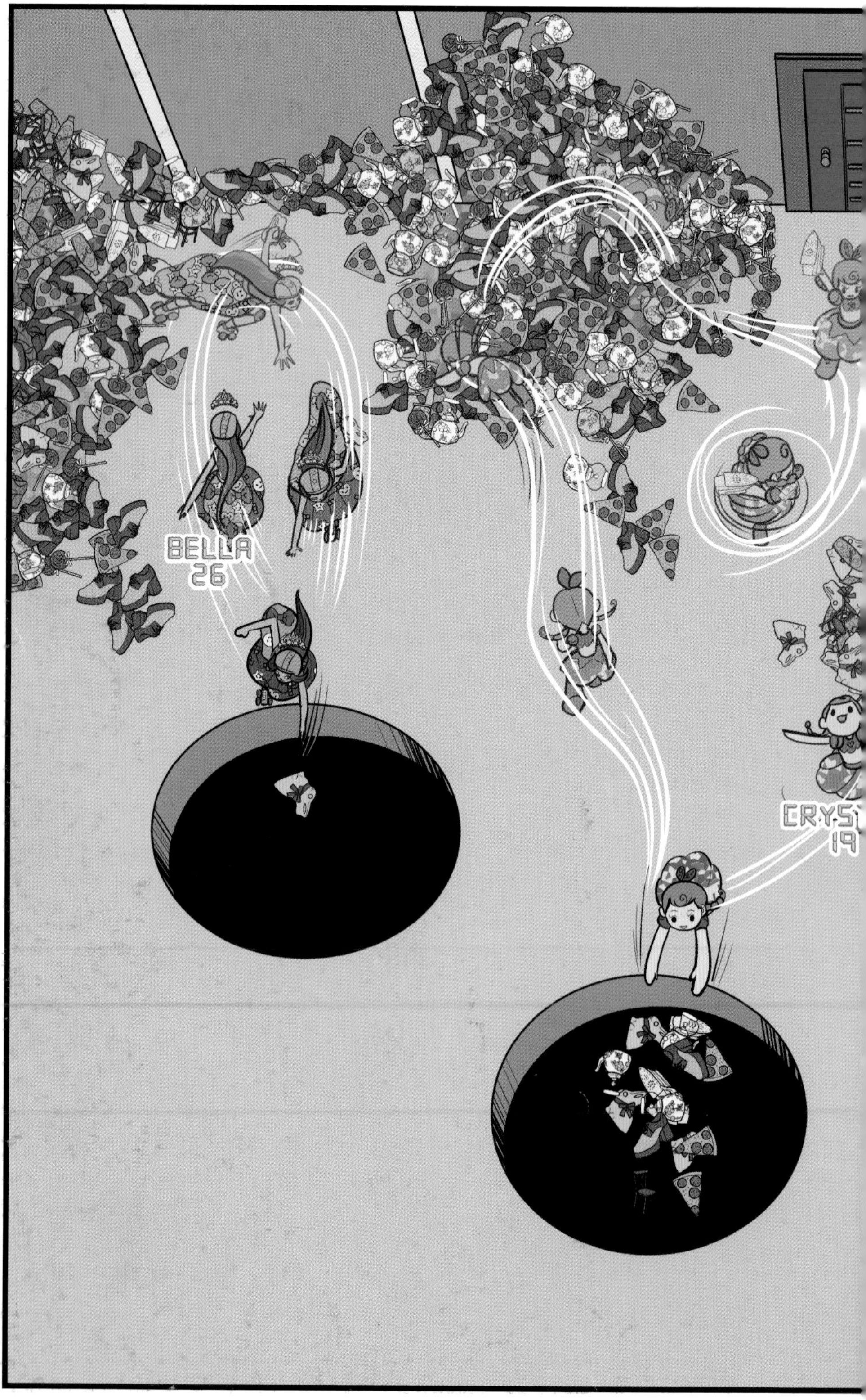
BELLA
26
CRYS
19

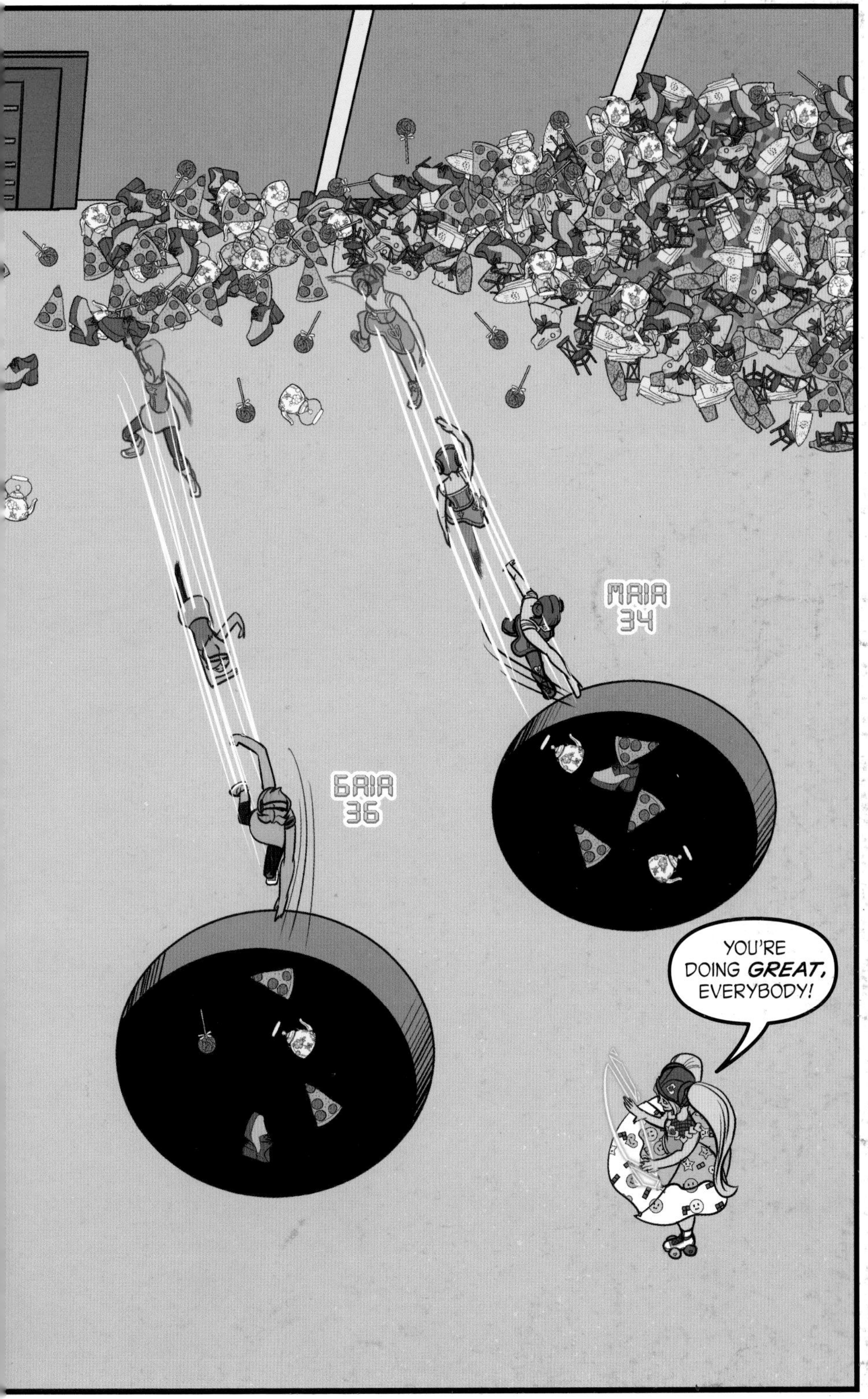
MAIA
34
GAIA
36
YOU'RE DOING **GREAT,** EVERYBODY!

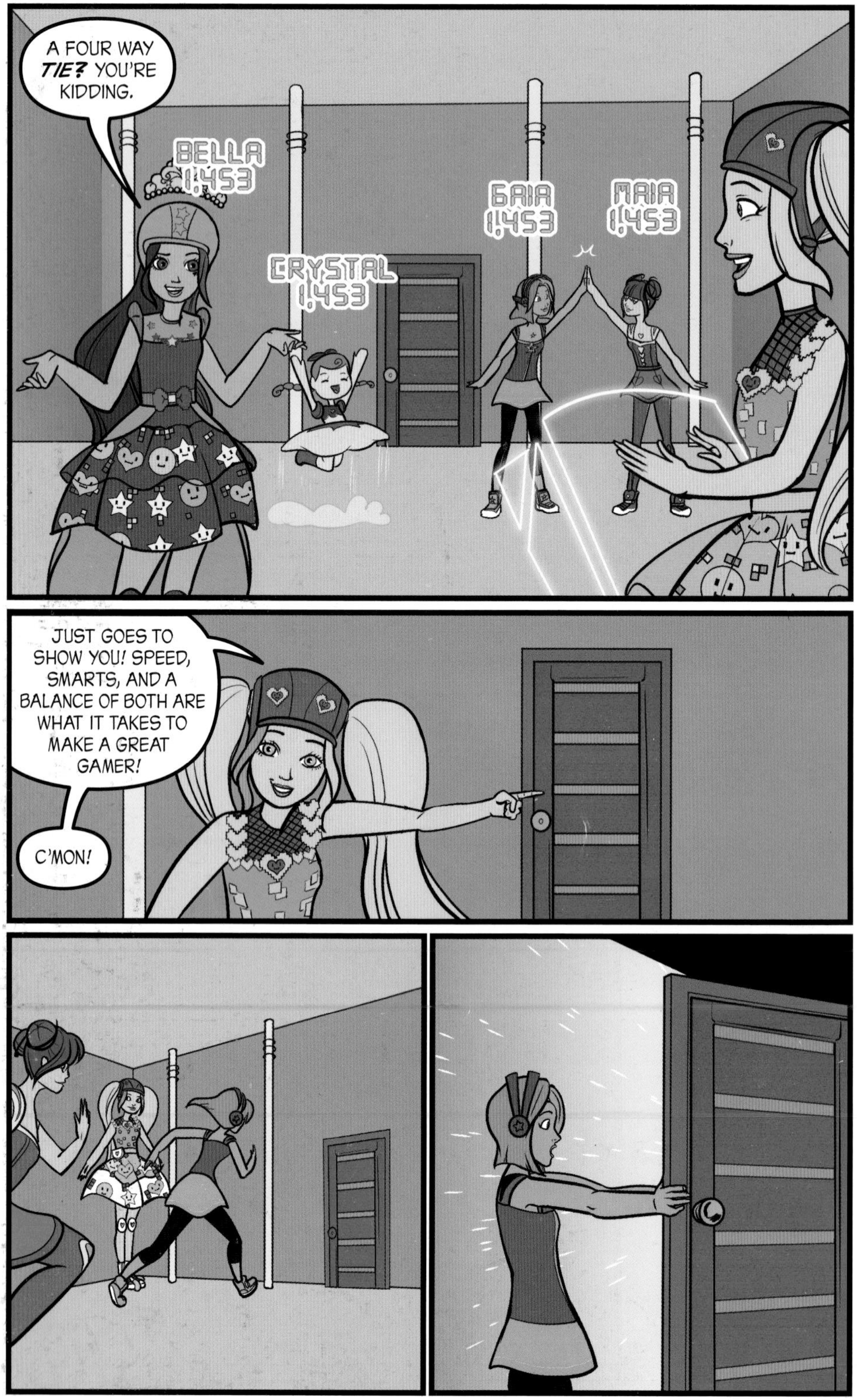
A FOUR WAY TIE? YOU'RE KIDDING.
BELLA 1,453
CRYSTAL 1,453
GAIA 1,453
MAIA 1,453
JUST GOES TO SHOW YOU! SPEED, SMARTS, AND A BALANCE OF BOTH ARE WHAT IT TAKES TO MAKE A GREAT GAMER!
C'MON!

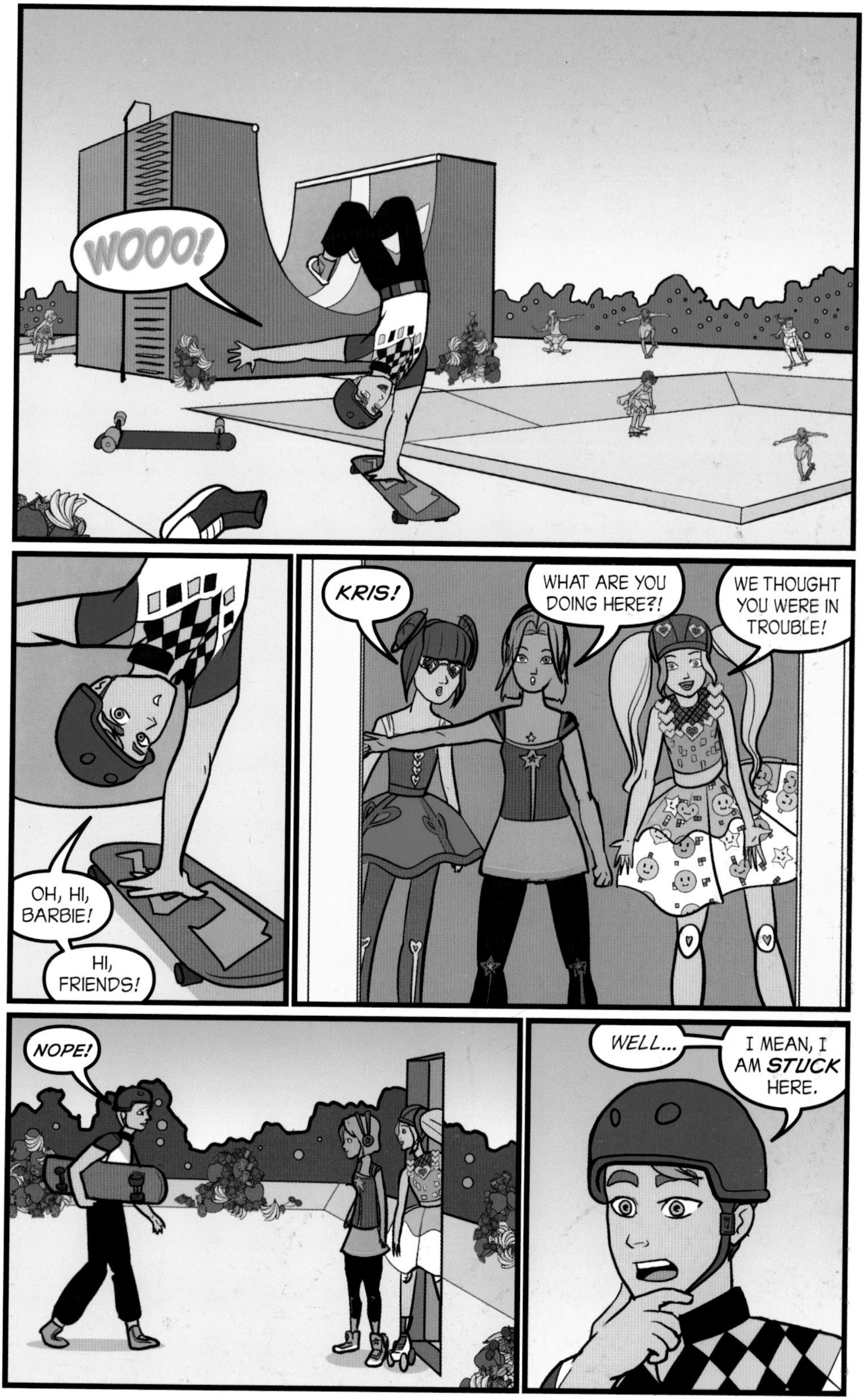
WOOO!
OH, HI, BARBIE!
HI, FRIENDS!
KRIS!
WHAT ARE YOU DOING HERE?!
WE THOUGHT YOU WERE IN TROUBLE!
NOPE!
WELL...
I MEAN, I AM STUCK HERE.

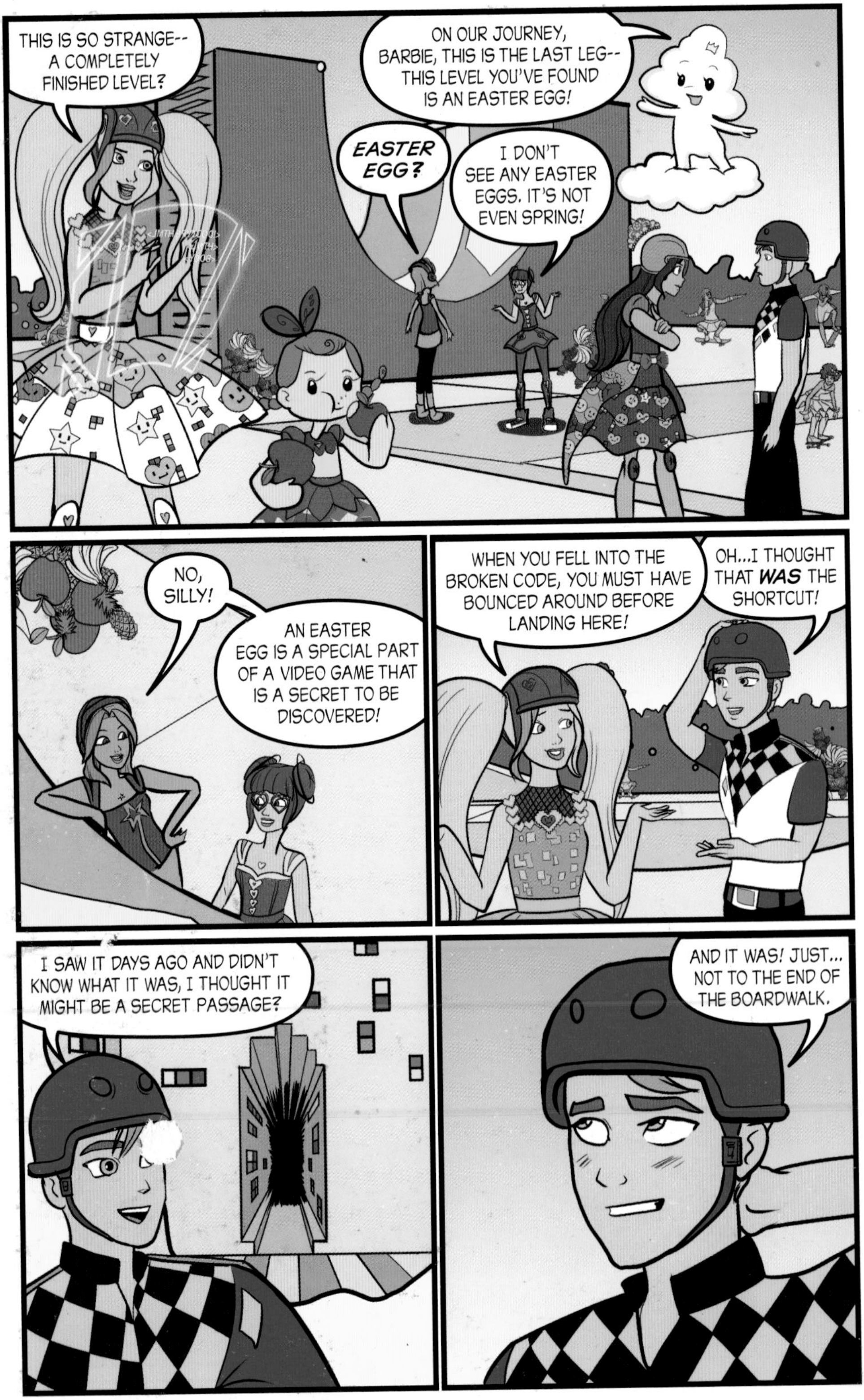
THIS IS SO STRANGE-- A COMPLETELY FINISHED LEVEL?
ON OUR JOURNEY, BARBIE, THIS IS THE LAST LEG-- THIS LEVEL YOU'VE FOUND IS AN EASTER EGG!
EASTER EGG?
I DON'T SEE ANY EASTER EGGS. IT'S NOT EVEN SPRING!
NO, SILLY!
AN EASTER EGG IS A SPECIAL PART OF A VIDEO GAME THAT IS A SECRET TO BE DISCOVERED!
WHEN YOU FELL INTO THE BROKEN CODE, YOU MUST HAVE BOUNCED AROUND BEFORE LANDING HERE!
OH...I THOUGHT THAT ***WAS*** THE SHORTCUT!
I SAW IT DAYS AGO AND DIDN'T KNOW WHAT IT WAS, I THOUGHT IT MIGHT BE A SECRET PASSAGE?
AND IT WAS! JUST... NOT TO THE END OF THE BOARDWALK.

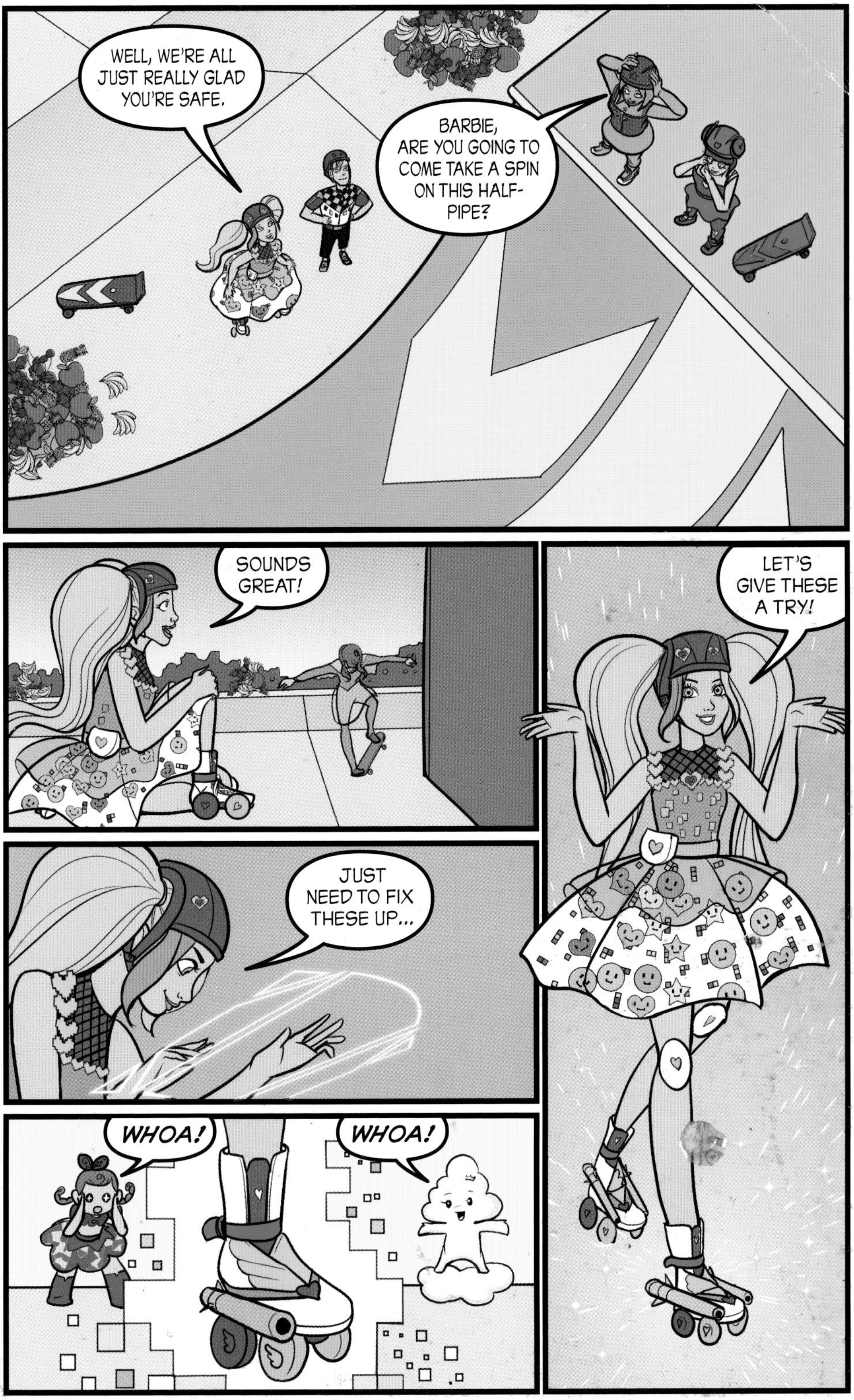
WELL, WE'RE ALL JUST REALLY GLAD YOU'RE SAFE.
BARBIE, ARE YOU GOING TO COME TAKE A SPIN ON THIS HALF-PIPE?
SOUNDS GREAT!
JUST NEED TO FIX THESE UP...
WHOA!
WHOA!
LET'S GIVE THESE A TRY!

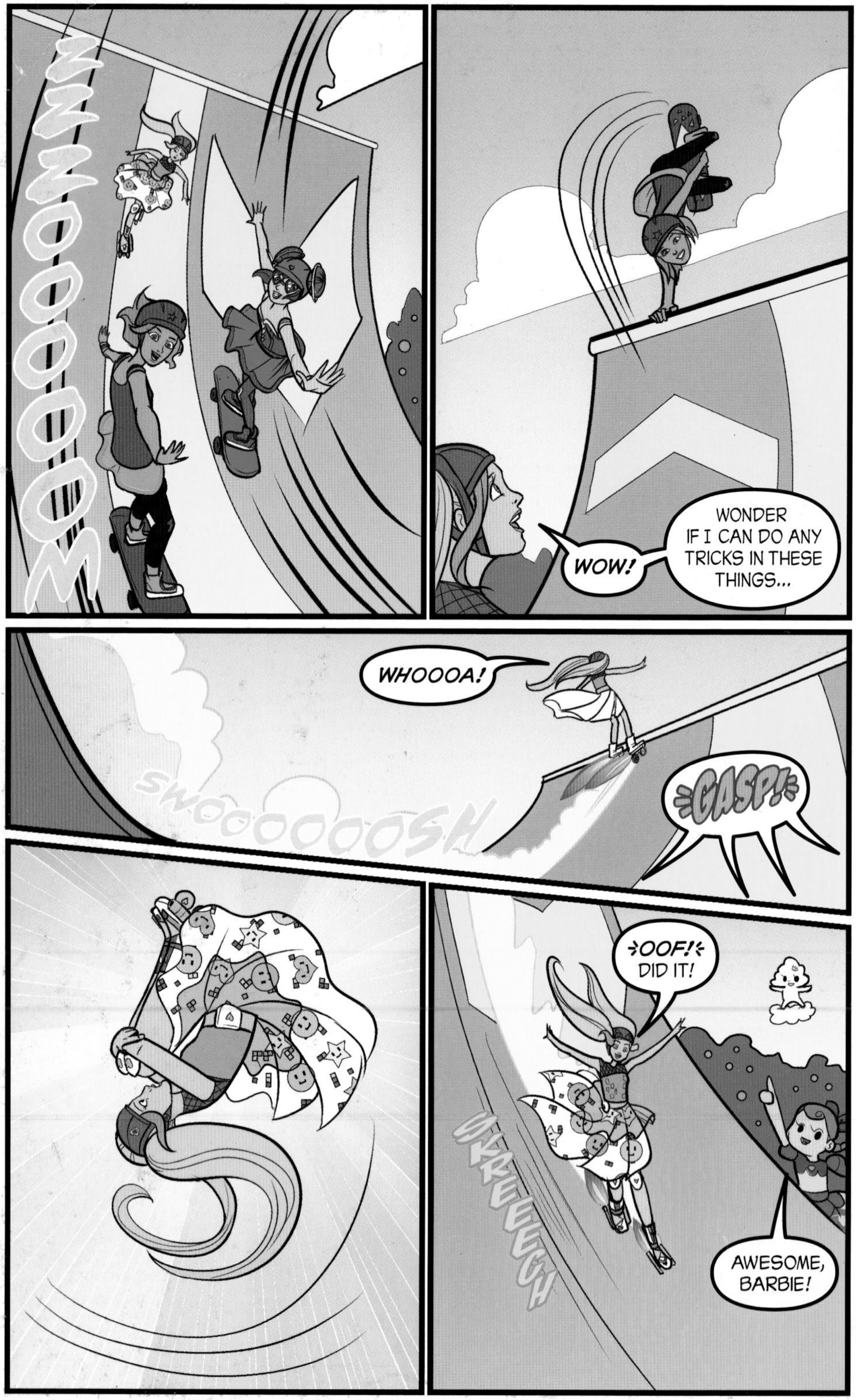
ZZZOOOOOOOOM
WOW!
WONDER IF I CAN DO ANY TRICKS IN THESE THINGS...
WHOOOA!
SWOOOOOOOOSH
GASP!
OOF! DID IT!
SKREEECH
AWESOME, BARBIE!

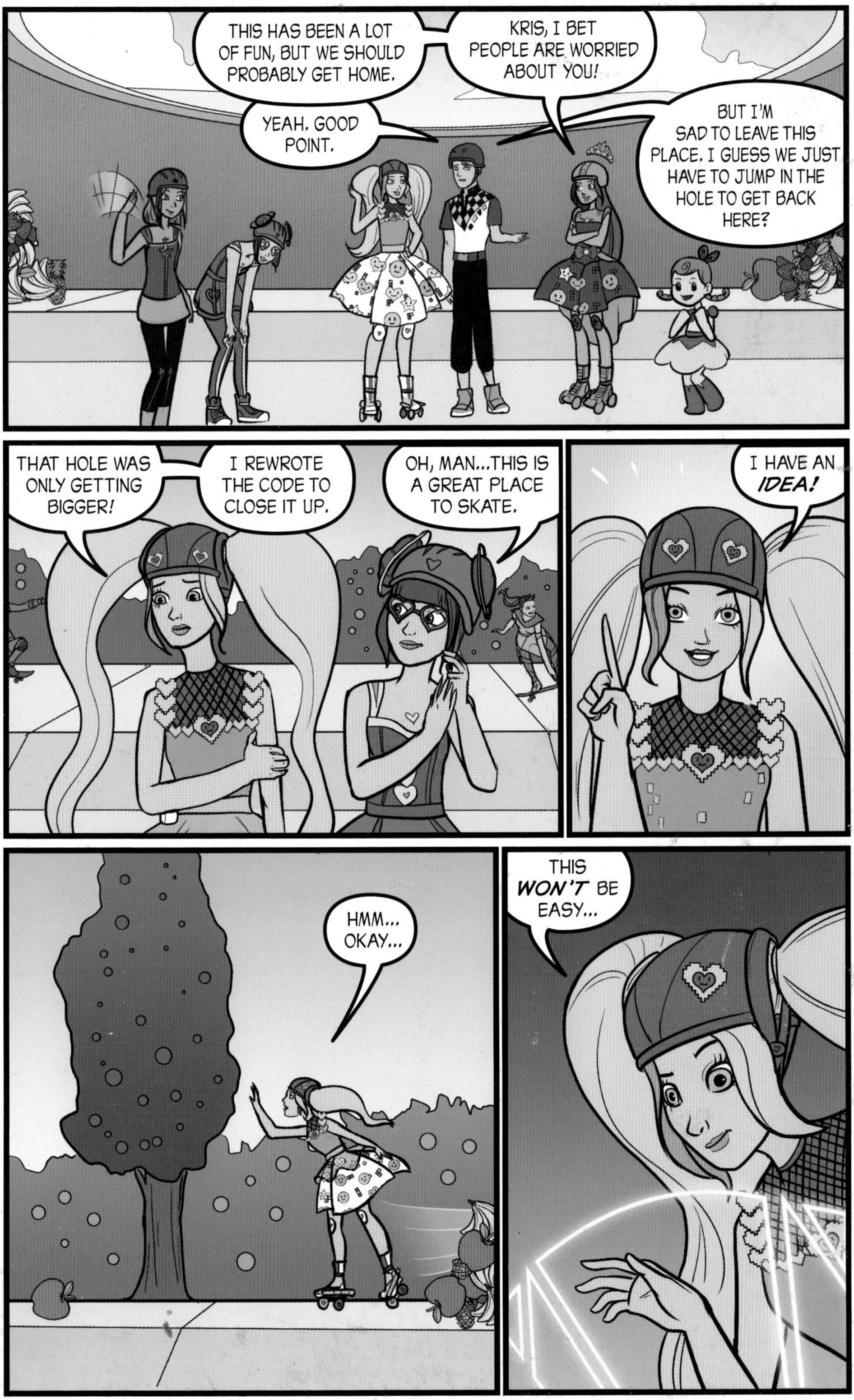
THIS HAS BEEN A LOT OF FUN, BUT WE SHOULD PROBABLY GET HOME.
KRIS, I BET PEOPLE ARE WORRIED ABOUT YOU!
YEAH. GOOD POINT.
BUT I'M SAD TO LEAVE THIS PLACE. I GUESS WE JUST HAVE TO JUMP IN THE HOLE TO GET BACK HERE?
THAT HOLE WAS ONLY GETTING BIGGER!
I REWROTE THE CODE TO CLOSE IT UP.
OH, MAN...THIS IS A GREAT PLACE TO SKATE.
I HAVE AN *IDEA!*
HMM... OKAY...
THIS *WON'T* BE EASY...

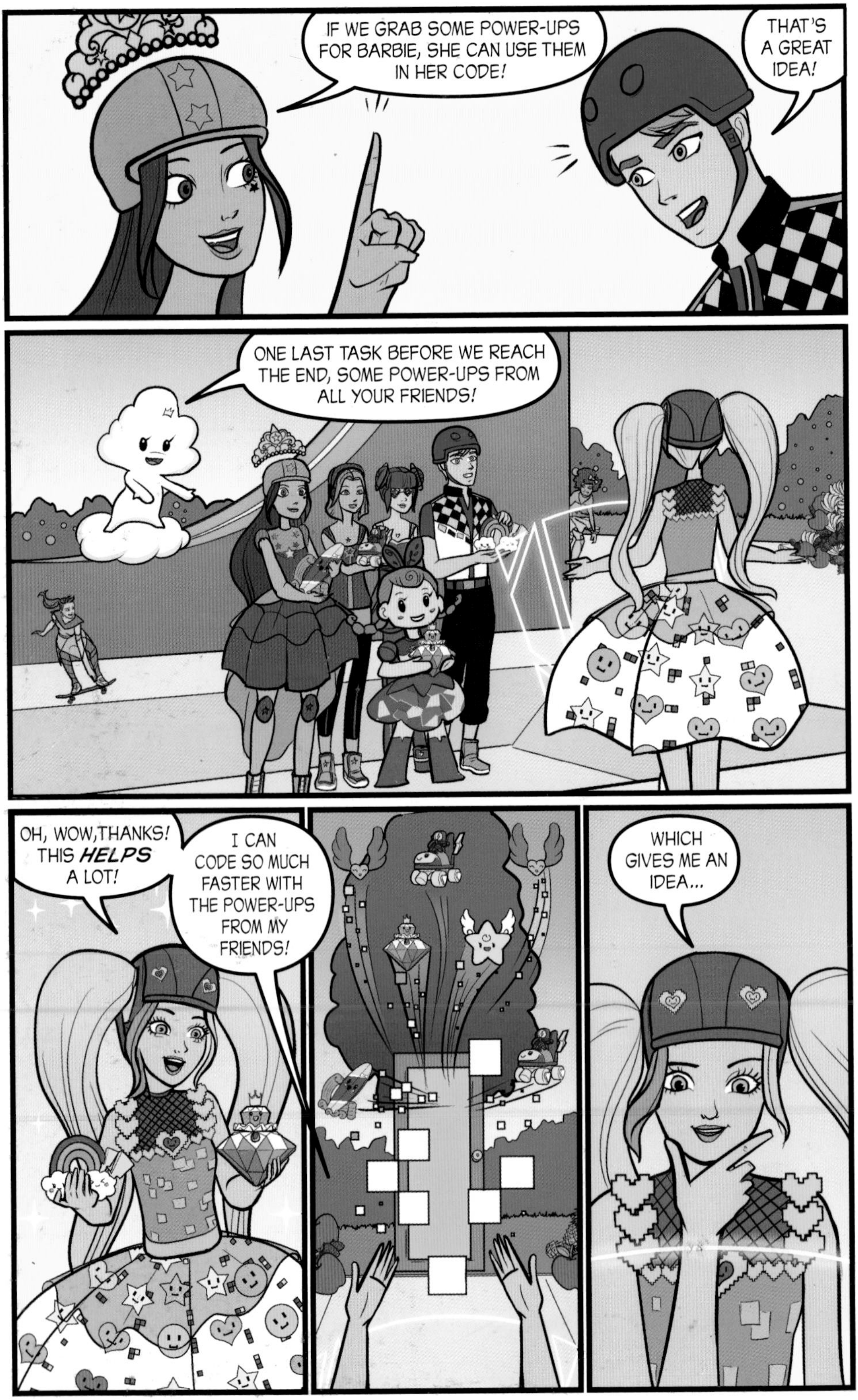
IF WE GRAB SOME POWER-UPS FOR BARBIE, SHE CAN USE THEM IN HER CODE!
THAT'S A GREAT IDEA!
ONE LAST TASK BEFORE WE REACH THE END, SOME POWER-UPS FROM ALL YOUR FRIENDS!
OH, WOW, THANKS! THIS **HELPS** A LOT!
I CAN CODE SO MUCH FASTER WITH THE POWER-UPS FROM MY FRIENDS!
WHICH GIVES ME AN IDEA...

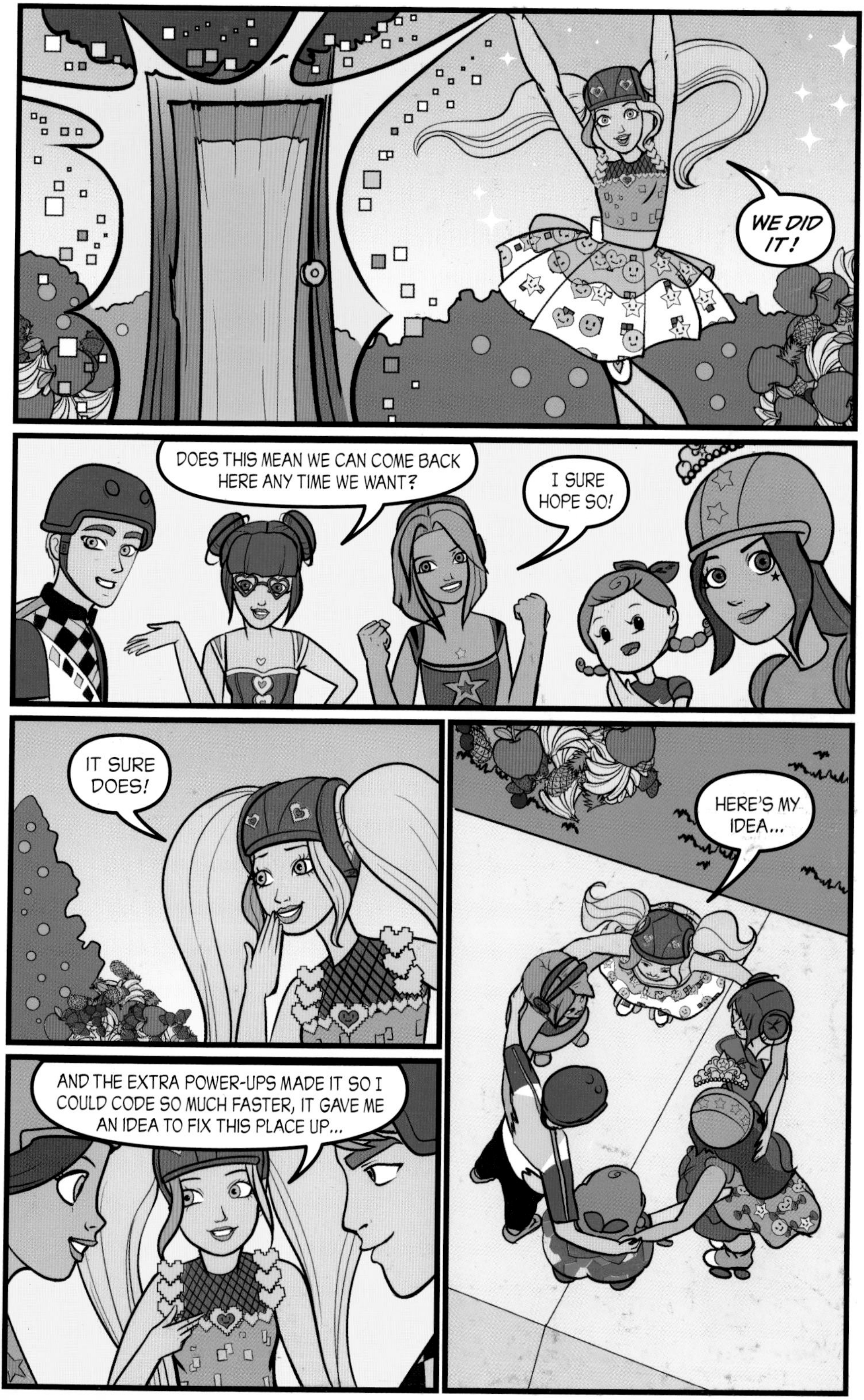
WE DID IT!
DOES THIS MEAN WE CAN COME BACK HERE ANY TIME WE WANT?
I SURE HOPE SO!
IT SURE DOES!
AND THE EXTRA POWER-UPS MADE IT SO I COULD CODE SO MUCH FASTER, IT GAVE ME AN IDEA TO FIX THIS PLACE UP...
HERE'S MY IDEA...

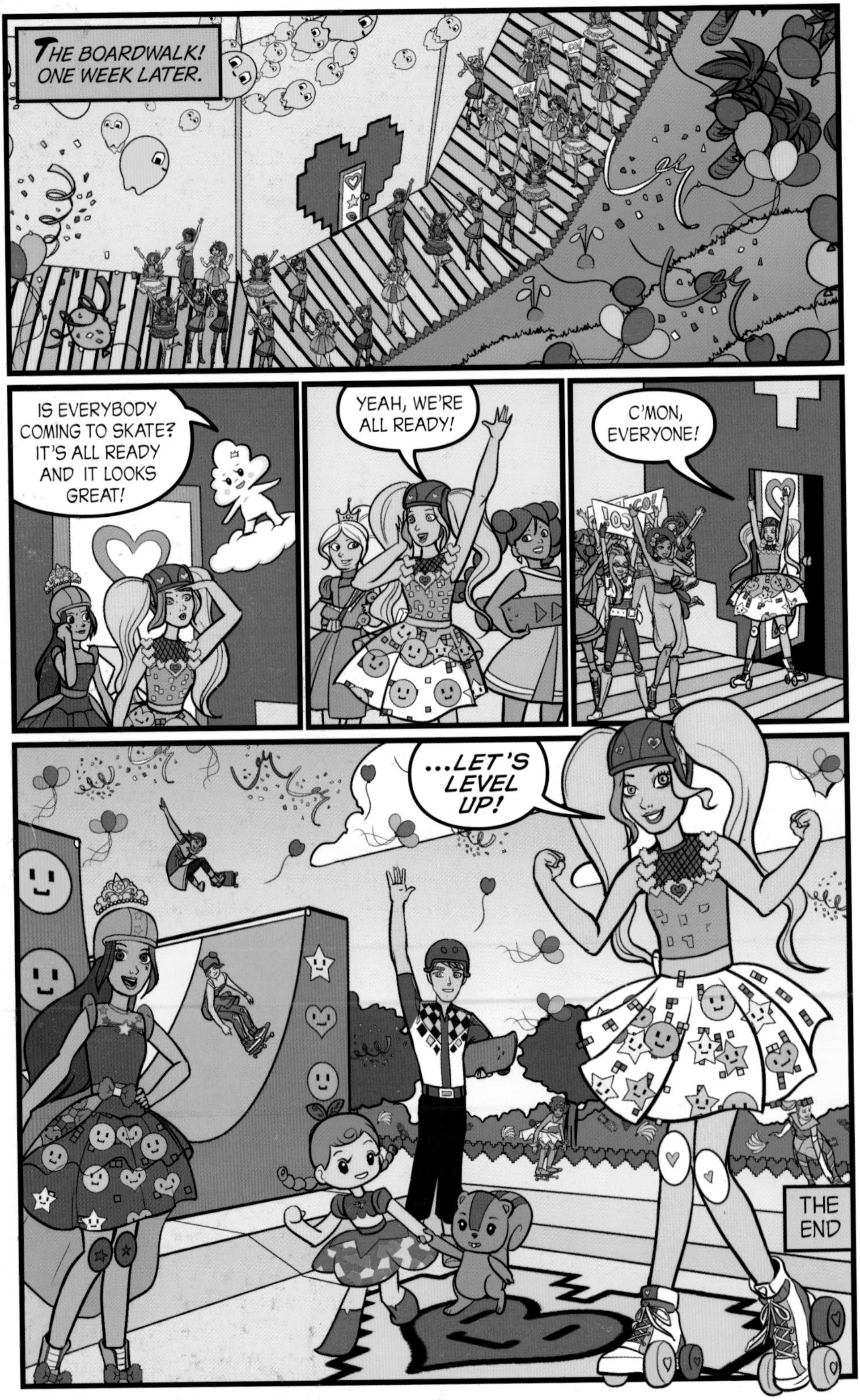
THE BOARDWALK! ONE WEEK LATER.
IS EVERYBODY COMING TO SKATE? IT'S ALL READY AND IT LOOKS GREAT!
YEAH, WE'RE ALL READY!
C'MON, EVERYONE!
...LET'S LEVEL UP!
THE END

# WATCH OUT FOR PAPERCUTZ

Welcome to the fast-paced, premiere BARBIE VIDEO GAME HERO graphic novel from Papercutz, for those fashionable video-game players dedicated to publishing great graphic novels for all ages. I'm Jim Salicrup, Editor-in-Chief , and I hope you enjoyed this all-new graphic novel, written by Tini Howard, and illustrated by Jules Rivera, inspired by the DVD starring Barbie, and featuring Chelsea, Crystal, Cutie, Gaia, Kris, Maia, Princess Bella, Renee, and Teresa .

If BARBIE VIDEO GAME HERO was your very first BARBIE graphic novel, and you enjoyed it, we have good news for you! There are several other BARBIE graphic novels from Papercutz available at your favorite bookseller or library that you may enjoy as well...

The first graphic novel is BARBIE #1 "Fashion Superstar," by Sarah Kuhn, writer, and Alitha Martinez, artist. Barbie dreams of a career in fashion, and she just got her first big break—assisting world-famous fashion designer Whitney Yang at her big Spring Fashion Show! But when things start going wrong, it's up to Barbie and her friends to work some fashion miracles.

In BARBIE #2 "Big Dreams, Best Friends," by Sarah Kuhn, writer, and Yishan Li, artist. Barbie continues on her fashion adventure, this time designing for one of the world's biggest pop stars. But when Barbie experiences designer's block and can't get in the stitch of things, helping out the shy drummer may get her back on track!

BARBIE PUPPY PARTY, by Danica Davidson, writer, and Maria Victoria Robado, artist. Not only does it star Barbie, it also features Barbie's sisters, Chelsea, Stacie, and Skipper, along with their pet puppies, Honey, Rookie, Taffy, and DJ! Barbie and her sisters are organizing an adoption event for the local animal shelter, but it's scheduled on the same day as the puppies' birthday. The Puppies think they're being forgotten, but that can't be, can it? The surprising answer awaits you within BARBIE PUPPY PARTY.

In BARBIE STAR LIGHT ADVENTURE, by Tini Howard, writer, and Jules Rivera, artist, the same creative team who brought you BARBIE VIDEO GAME HERO, Barbie, in this special graphic novel, is Princess Star Light, from the planet Para-Den. When she discovers someone is trying to destroy the environment, Barbie and her friends, Sal-Lee (a hoverboard racing legend), Sheena and Kareena (Gravity Geniuses), and Leo (Prince and pilot) work together to save the planet they love.

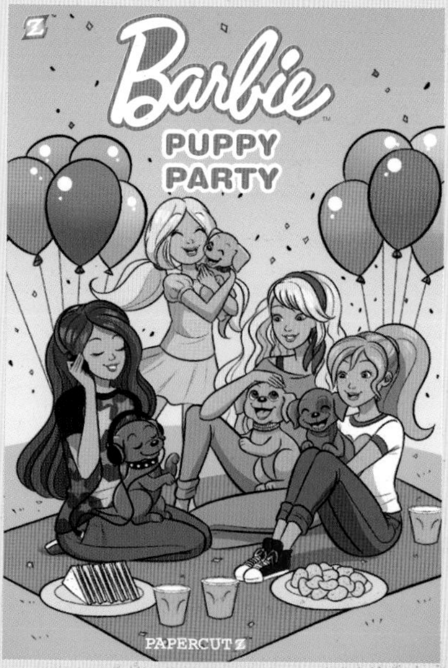
Barbie
PUPPY PARTY
PAPERCUTZ

And there are more great BARBIE graphic novels to come! We don't want you to miss out on any of the great BARBIE comics, so for more news about upcoming BARBIE graphic novels, be sure to visit Papercutz.com.

Thanks,

Jim

**STAY IN TOUCH!**

EMAIL: salicrup@papercutz.com
WEB: papercutz.com
INSTAGRAM: @papercutzgn
TWITTER: @papercutzgn
FACEBOOK: PAPERCUTZGRAPHICNOVELS
FANMAIL: Papercutz, 160 Broadway, Suite 700
East Wing, New York, NY 10038

## Special Preview of BARBIE #2

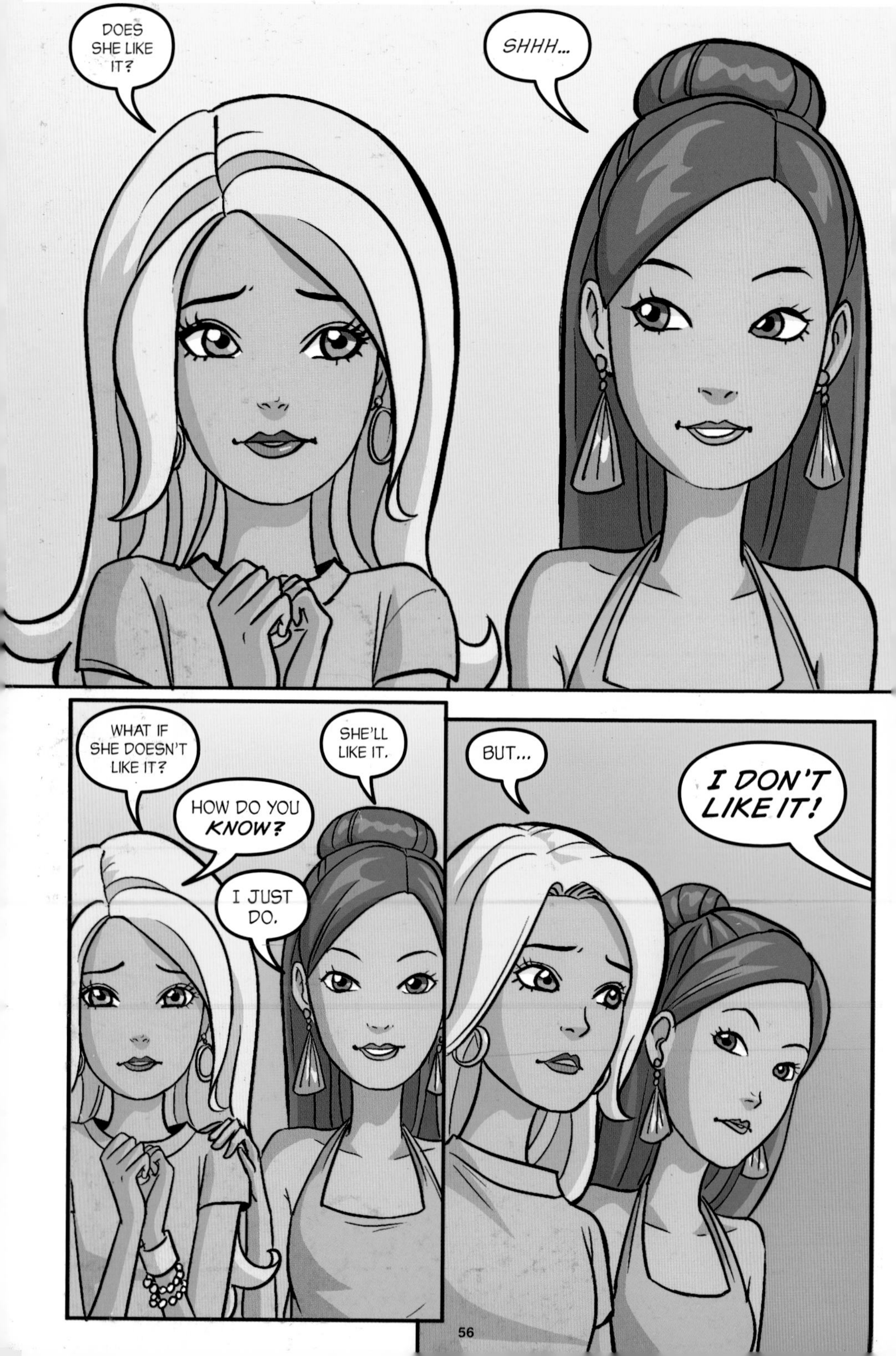
DOES SHE LIKE IT?
SHHH...
WHAT IF SHE DOESN'T LIKE IT?
SHE'LL LIKE IT.
HOW DO YOU *KNOW?*
I JUST DO.
BUT...
*I DON'T LIKE IT!*

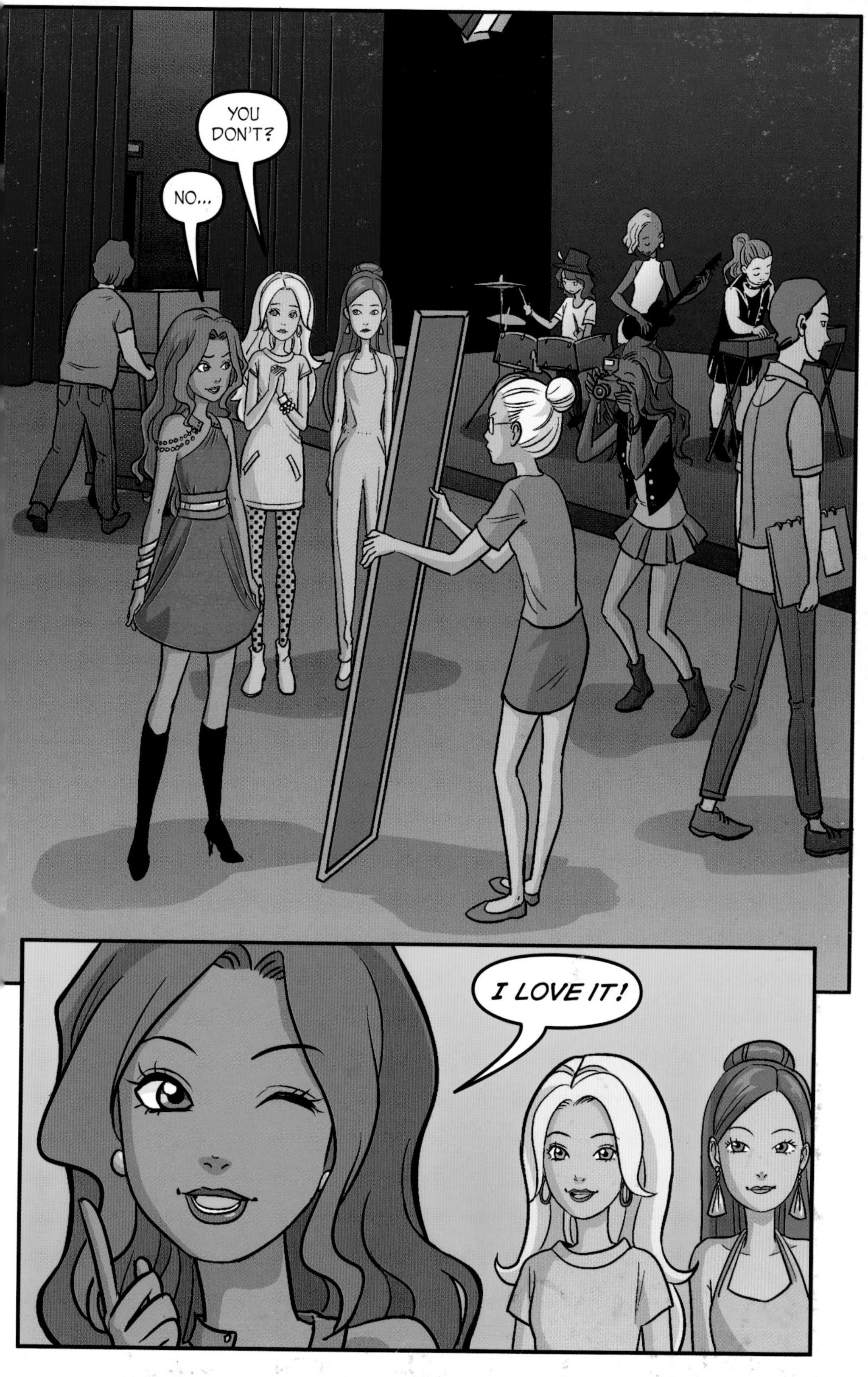
NO...
YOU DON'T?
I LOVE IT!

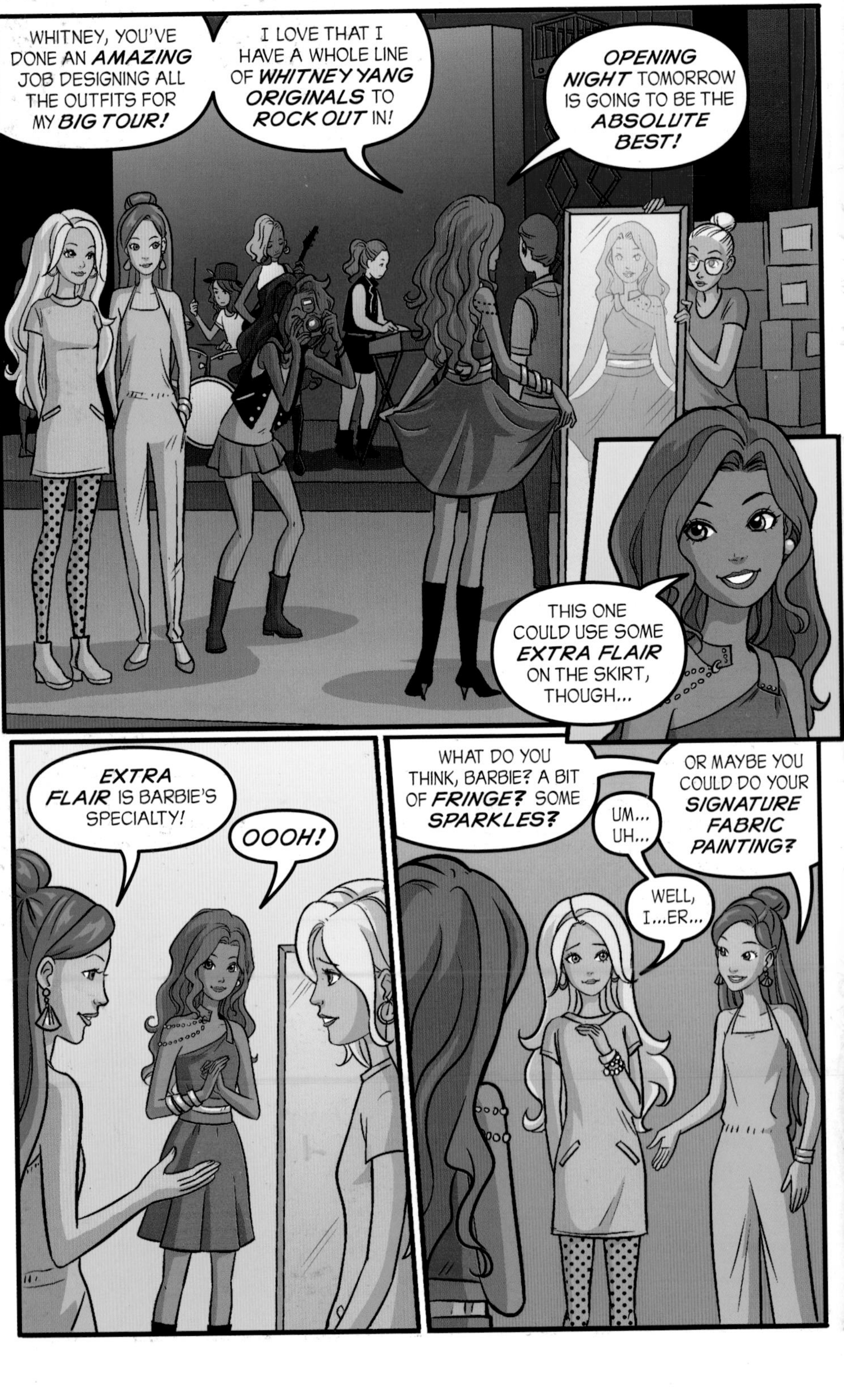

WHITNEY, YOU'VE DONE AN AMAZING JOB DESIGNING ALL THE OUTFITS FOR MY BIG TOUR!
I LOVE THAT I HAVE A WHOLE LINE OF WHITNEY YANG ORIGINALS TO ROCK OUT IN!
OPENING NIGHT TOMORROW IS GOING TO BE THE ABSOLUTE BEST!
THIS ONE COULD USE SOME EXTRA FLAIR ON THE SKIRT, THOUGH...
EXTRA FLAIR IS BARBIE'S SPECIALTY!
OOOH!
WHAT DO YOU THINK, BARBIE? A BIT OF FRINGE? SOME SPARKLES?
UM... UH...
OR MAYBE YOU COULD DO YOUR SIGNATURE FABRIC PAINTING?
WELL, I...ER...

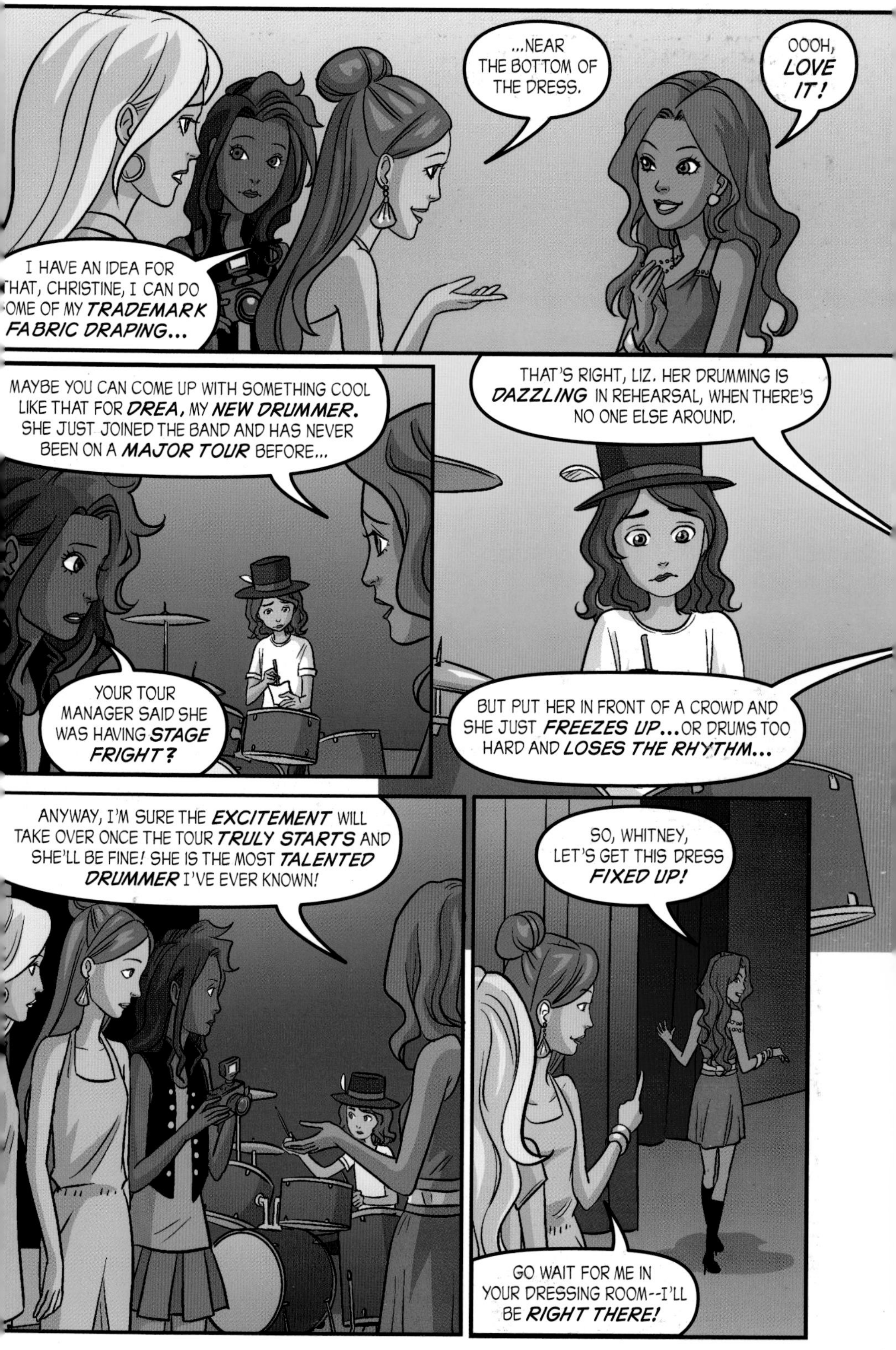
...NEAR THE BOTTOM OF THE DRESS.
I HAVE AN IDEA FOR THAT, CHRISTINE, I CAN DO SOME OF MY TRADEMARK FABRIC DRAPING...
OOOH, LOVE IT!
MAYBE YOU CAN COME UP WITH SOMETHING COOL LIKE THAT FOR DREA, MY NEW DRUMMER. SHE JUST JOINED THE BAND AND HAS NEVER BEEN ON A MAJOR TOUR BEFORE...
YOUR TOUR MANAGER SAID SHE WAS HAVING STAGE FRIGHT?
THAT'S RIGHT, LIZ. HER DRUMMING IS DAZZLING IN REHEARSAL, WHEN THERE'S NO ONE ELSE AROUND.
BUT PUT HER IN FRONT OF A CROWD AND SHE JUST FREEZES UP...OR DRUMS TOO HARD AND LOSES THE RHYTHM...
ANYWAY, I'M SURE THE EXCITEMENT WILL TAKE OVER ONCE THE TOUR TRULY STARTS AND SHE'LL BE FINE! SHE IS THE MOST TALENTED DRUMMER I'VE EVER KNOWN!
SO, WHITNEY, LET'S GET THIS DRESS FIXED UP!
GO WAIT FOR ME IN YOUR DRESSING ROOM--I'LL BE RIGHT THERE!

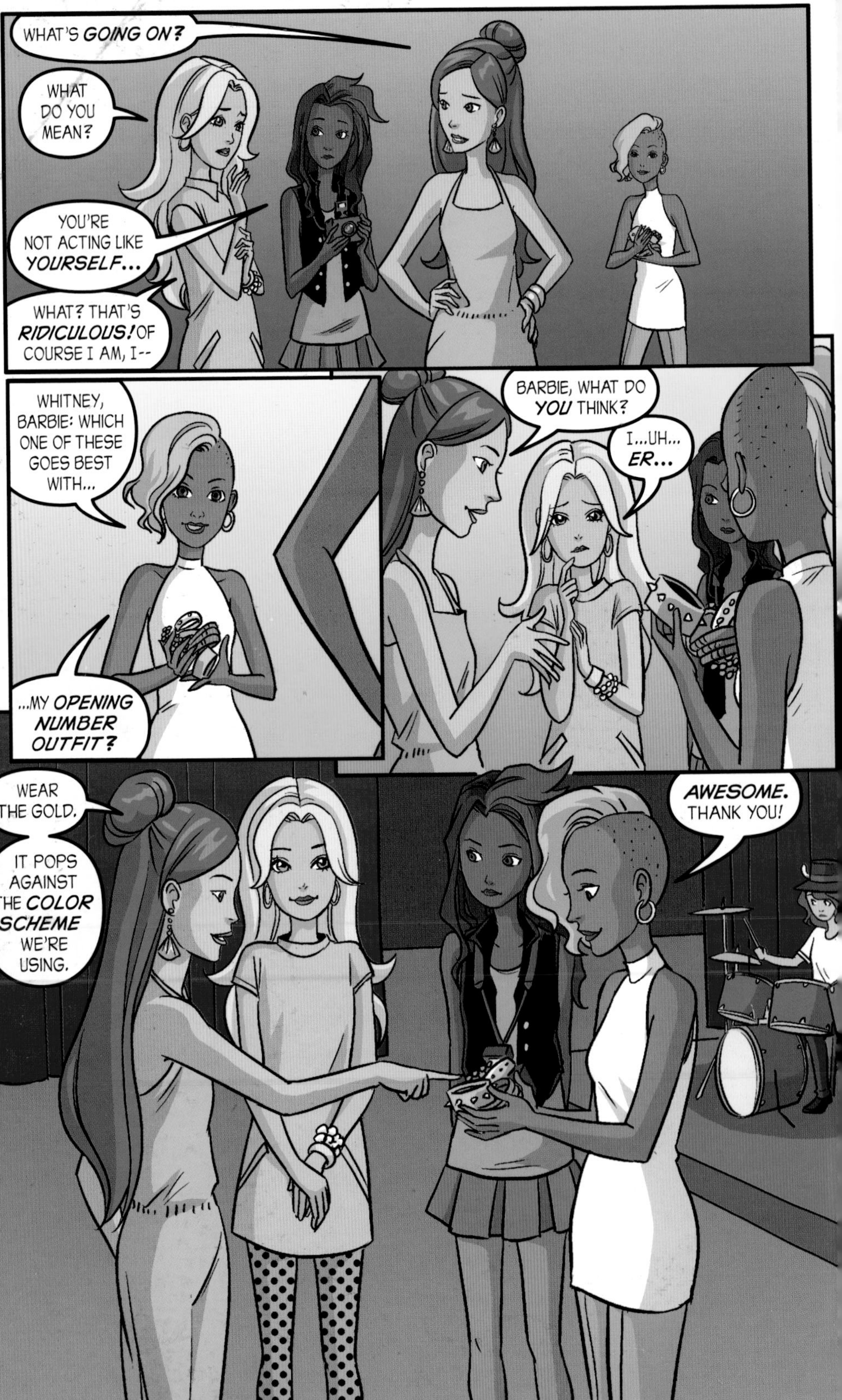

WHAT'S **GOING ON?**
WHAT DO YOU MEAN?
YOU'RE NOT ACTING LIKE **YOURSELF...**
WHAT? THAT'S **RIDICULOUS!** OF COURSE I AM, I--
WHITNEY, BARBIE: WHICH ONE OF THESE GOES BEST WITH...
...MY **OPENING NUMBER OUTFIT?**
BARBIE, WHAT DO **YOU** THINK?
I...UH... **ER...**
WEAR THE GOLD.
IT POPS AGAINST THE **COLOR SCHEME** WE'RE USING.
**AWESOME.** THANK YOU!

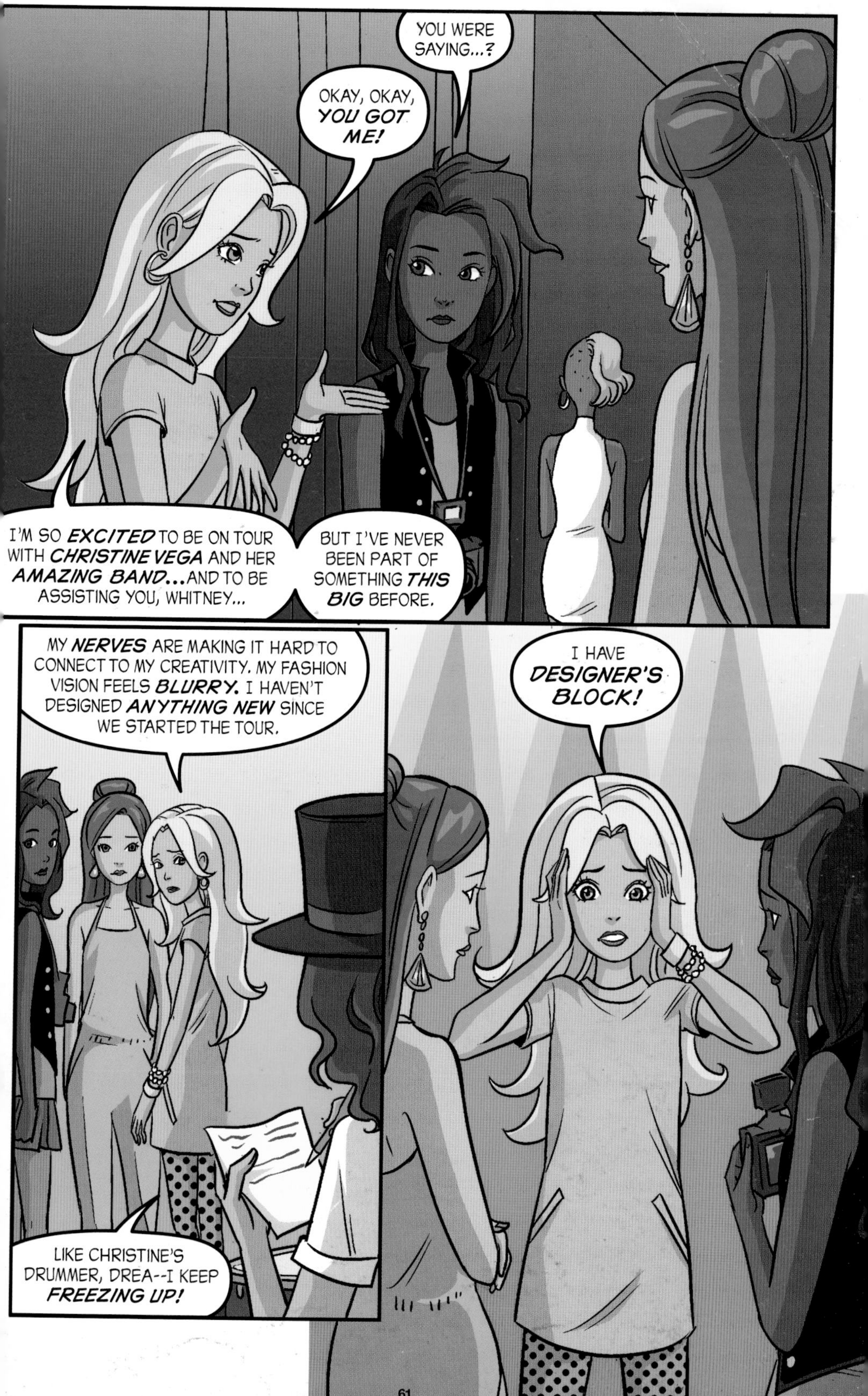
YOU WERE SAYING...?
OKAY, OKAY, *YOU GOT ME!*
I'M SO *EXCITED* TO BE ON TOUR WITH *CHRISTINE VEGA* AND HER *AMAZING BAND...*AND TO BE ASSISTING YOU, WHITNEY...
BUT I'VE NEVER BEEN PART OF SOMETHING *THIS BIG* BEFORE.
MY *NERVES* ARE MAKING IT HARD TO CONNECT TO MY CREATIVITY. MY FASHION VISION FEELS *BLURRY.* I HAVEN'T DESIGNED *ANYTHING NEW* SINCE WE STARTED THE TOUR.
LIKE CHRISTINE'S DRUMMER, DREA--I KEEP *FREEZING UP!*
I HAVE *DESIGNER'S BLOCK!*

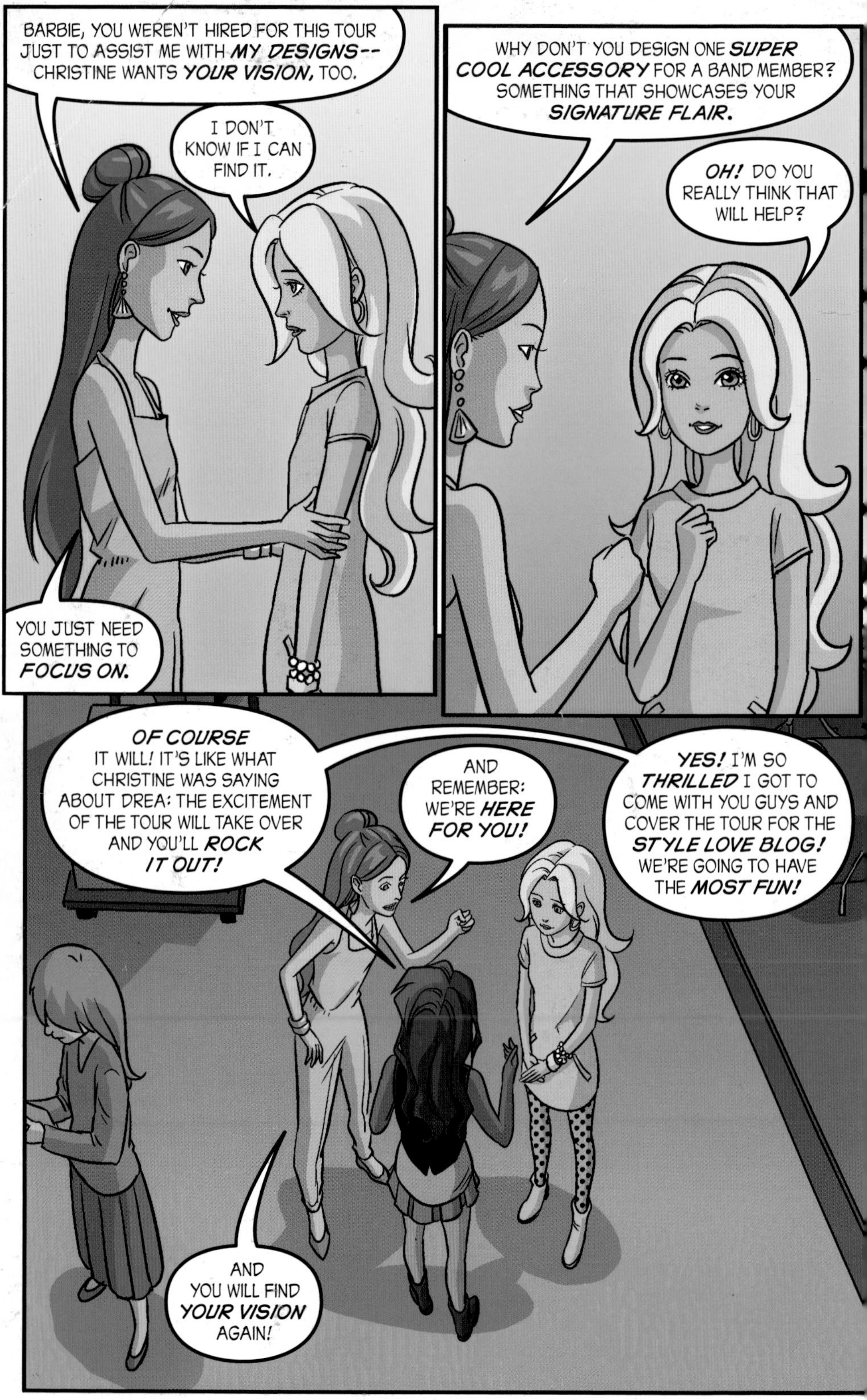
BARBIE, YOU WEREN'T HIRED FOR THIS TOUR JUST TO ASSIST ME WITH MY DESIGNS-- CHRISTINE WANTS YOUR VISION, TOO.
I DON'T KNOW IF I CAN FIND IT.
YOU JUST NEED SOMETHING TO FOCUS ON.
WHY DON'T YOU DESIGN ONE SUPER COOL ACCESSORY FOR A BAND MEMBER? SOMETHING THAT SHOWCASES YOUR SIGNATURE FLAIR.
OH! DO YOU REALLY THINK THAT WILL HELP?
OF COURSE IT WILL! IT'S LIKE WHAT CHRISTINE WAS SAYING ABOUT DREA: THE EXCITEMENT OF THE TOUR WILL TAKE OVER AND YOU'LL ROCK IT OUT!
AND REMEMBER: WE'RE HERE FOR YOU!
YES! I'M SO THRILLED I GOT TO COME WITH YOU GUYS AND COVER THE TOUR FOR THE STYLE LOVE BLOG! WE'RE GOING TO HAVE THE MOST FUN!
AND YOU WILL FIND YOUR VISION AGAIN!

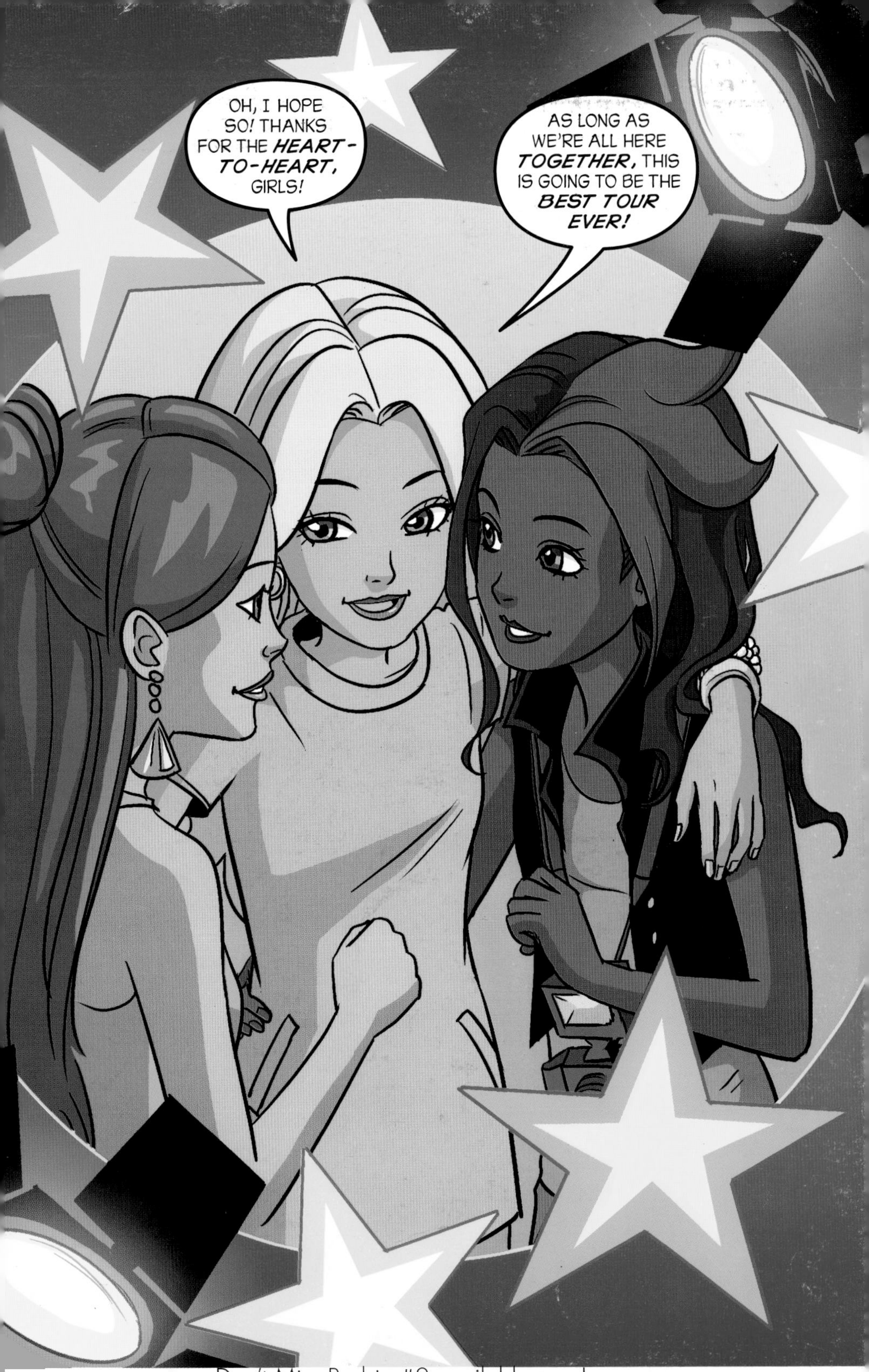
OH, I HOPE SO! THANKS FOR THE *HEART-TO-HEART,* GIRLS!
AS LONG AS WE'RE ALL HERE *TOGETHER,* THIS IS GOING TO BE THE *BEST TOUR EVER!*

ADVERTISEMENT

Harris County Public Library
Houston, Texas

# STORY OF Barbie ™

## AND THE WOMAN WHO CREATED HER

On Sale 9/5/17

BARBIE and associated trademarks and trade dress are owned by and used under license from, Mattel © 2017 Mattel. All rights reserved.

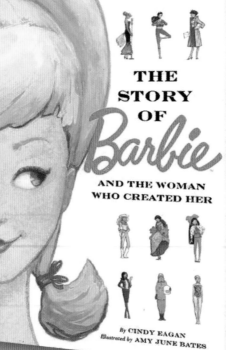

THE STORY OF Barbie ™

AND THE WOMAN WHO CREATED HER

By CINDY EAGAN
Illustrated by AMY JUNE BATES

## Discover the true story of the world's most famous doll.

RHCB

## Visit BarbieBooks.com to order your copy!